THE
WEDDING
THAT ALMOST
WASN'T

D1536308

THE
WEDDING
THAT ALMOST
WASN'T

CHERIE BENNETT

AN
APPLE
PAPERBACK

SCHOLASTIC INC.
New York   Toronto   London   Auckland   Sydney

To the younger sisters of my longtime readers who are now reading my books: Thank your older sister(s) for me, and welcome to the sisterhood!

If you purchased this book without a cover, you should be aware that this book is stolen property. It was reported as "unsold and destroyed" to the publisher, and neither the author nor the publisher has received any payment for this "stripped book."

No part of this publication may be reproduced in whole or in part, or stored in a retrieval system, or transmitted in any form or by any means, electronic, mechanical, photocopying, recording, or otherwise, without written permission of the publisher. For information regarding permission, write to Scholastic Inc., Attention: Permissions Department, 555 Broadway, New York, NY 10012.

ISBN 0-590-05959-9

Copyright © 1998 by Cherie Bennett. All rights reserved. Published by Scholastic Inc. SCHOLASTIC and logos are trademarks and/or registered trademarks of Scholastic Inc. APPLE PAPERBACKS and the APPLE PAPERBACKS logo are trademarks and/or registered trademarks of Scholastic Inc.

12 11 10 9 8 7 6 5 4 3 2 1   8 9/9 0 1 2 3/0

Printed in the U.S.A.   40
First Scholastic printing, July 1998

1

"This is a very, very special, sacred occasion," Brianna Zeeman — everyone called her Breezy — solemnly told her two best friends, Cassie Pearson and Annie McGee.

"Yeah, for once you didn't finish all the popcorn before I got any," Annie joked, reaching over for a handful and stuffing it into her mouth.

Breezy loved junk food, and her friends were always teasing her about it. "I hardly ate any," she protested, embarrassed.

"Breezy — I'm joking," Annie assured her. She threw a kernel of popcorn into the air and opened her mouth wide to catch it.

"Come on, Annie," Cassie pleaded. "This is important. Stop eating."

"Okay, okay," Annie agreed, leaning back against one of the huge pillows on the floor, but not before she took a piece of bubble gum out of her back pocket, unwrapped it, and popped it into her mouth. "If I can't eat, at least I can chew."

"You can chew," Breezy agreed. "But don't pop any loud bubbles." She took a deep breath before continuing.

"We are here for a very special ceremony in our new clubhouse," she said. "It's — "

"A ceremony of trust and love between the three of us," Cassie continued dramatically.

Breezy nodded. "Best friends forever."

"Yeah, forever," Annie agreed, chewing her gum hard. "Or until we have some huge fight."

"Annie!" Cassie admonished her.

"I'm *joking*," Annie insisted.

Cassie looked relieved. "For a second there I thought you meant it."

"You guys, no fight could ever come between us," Breezy said. "*Nothing* can come between us."

Cassie smiled dreamily. "One day we'll all be in each other's weddings. And we'll buy houses right near each other."

"But not here in Summerville," Annie said. "No way, no how, not me."

"I love Summerville!" Cassie exclaimed. "I wouldn't ever want to leave!"

Breezy groaned. "We can worry about all that ten years from now, okay?"

Breezy was used to being the referee between Annie and Cassie. The three of them had been best friends for years, but they were all very different from one another, in both looks and personality. Breezy was tall, with a pretty, round face

2

and fine, shoulder-length brown hair. She thought her ears stuck out, and it made her very self-conscious. She got the best grades of the three of them, and she was a natural leader. She also got stressed out if she wasn't perfect.

Annie, on the other hand, didn't like school much at all, and she never seemed to get stressed out. She lived for sports and adventure — the more dangerous the better. The funny thing was, she didn't look like an athlete at all. Annie was quite short and at twelve was definitely a lot curvier than her two best friends (a fact that she hated). She also had beautiful curly red hair. Most of the time, it was stuck up under a baseball cap.

Cassie's glossy black hair was cut into a chin-length bob. She had huge eyes that peeked out from under her bangs. Cassie was smart, but sometimes she seemed naive to her friends, as if she were stuck in some kind of romantic dream world. Ever since Breezy and Annie had known her — which was to say, ever since the three of them started preschool together — Cassie had loved anything romantic. For example, when they were little, she always wanted to play "wedding," and she always wanted to be the bride.

And yet, despite their differences, Annie and Breezy and Cassie loved one another. A lot. In their small town of Summerville, Indiana, which was a suburb north of Indianapolis, every kid their age knew that where you found Breezy, you also found Annie and Cassie.

That's just the way it was.

Breezy looked at her two best friends, her eyes shining. "And now we have a special, secret place that belongs totally to us, and no one else," she intoned solemnly.

The girls were up in the attic at Breezy's house. Until nine months ago, it had been Breezy's older sister Liza's bedroom. But then Liza, who was a senior in college in Indianapolis, had gotten her own apartment with some friends. Breezy had begged for weeks to be allowed to turn the attic into a special hangout for her and her friends, and her parents had finally said yes. And then they offered to give her all the supplies she'd need to make the attic the girls' own.

Breezy, Cassie, and Annie had spent months redoing the attic, turning it into exactly what they wanted it to be. Now it was painted sky blue, with remnants of various carpet samples covering the wooden floor. Huge pillows that the girls had found at a secondhand store were strewn everywhere. And Breezy had brought up her CD player and all her CDs.

Just recently, the girls had hit a gold mine. Breezy's grandmother had moved from Indiana to a condominium in Florida, and she'd given Breezy all kinds of great stuff for their clubhouse. Standing near the small window was an old dress form, wearing her grandmother's actual wedding gown. Nails in the walls now held a variety of her grandmother's old hats and scarves, and some of her costume jewelry was hung up there as well.

But best of all was the hope chest.

It had been in Breezy's family for many generations, her grandmother had explained. And Breezy should only place very, very, very special things in it.

Just a couple of days earlier, Breezy and her friends had painted the chest the same blue as the walls, then dusted it with silver and gold glitter paint. They agreed that when the hope chest was completely dry, they would have a special ceremony, and they would each put something really personal that they deeply cherished inside it.

Only the three of them would know what was inside the chest. And they would each wear a key to the chest around their necks on a silver chain.

And now they were ready for their ceremony. Just yesterday, Breezy's mom had had the keys made for them. Breezy passed the keys out, and the girls put them on special silver chains they had purchased by saving up their allowance money.

"I love it," Cassie said happily, looking down at the key that hung just below her collarbone.

"I'll have to take it off for sports and stuff," Annie reminded them.

"That's okay," Breezy said. "As long as you put it right back on afterward."

Cassie looked at her two best friends. "So, who's going first?"

"I will," Annie said, scrambling to her feet. She took a much-folded photo, torn out of a magazine, out of her back pocket. The photo was of a woman giving a thumbs-up sign in front of an old-fashioned airplane.

"Who is that?" Cassie asked, baffled.

"Amelia Earhart," Annie said. "She was an aviatrix."

"What's that?" Cassie asked.

"A flyer, a woman flyer," Annie explained. "She was the first woman to try to fly solo around the world."

"Did she succeed?" Cassie asked.

"No, she disappeared over the Pacific," Annie admitted. "And no one ever found her. But someday I'm going to fly solo around the world. And this picture is to remind me that I'm going to succeed. No one knows about this but you guys. I mean, you know what it's like if you tell people. They, like, laugh at your dreams, you know?"

Breezy nodded. "We would never laugh, though."

"I know," Annie said. She lifted the top of the hope chest and carefully laid the photo inside. "Who's next?"

"I'll go," Breezy said. She opened her backpack and carefully took out a small glass dome.

Inside the dome was the figure of a dolphin jumping into the air. When Breezy shook the glass dome, tiny silver stars flew around inside the glass and fell gracefully onto the simulated ocean floor below as the liquid in the dome sloshed from side to side.

"My grandmother got this for me at Sea World in Florida," Breezy said, shaking the glass dome again to make the silver stars dance. "Someday I'm going to be a famous scientist, and I'm going to work with dolphins and learn their language — they can speak, you know."

"Really?" Cassie asked, wide-eyed.

Breezy nodded. "Someday I'm going to be able to talk to them in their language. And I'm going to invent a way to talk to them underwater, too." She carefully placed the glass dome into the hope chest.

"You know," Breezy continued, "once I started to tell my dad about how I was going to talk to dolphins, and I could tell he thought it was stupid. You know how it is — when your parents want to tell you that your idea is dumb, but they know that isn't what they're supposed to do, so they just get this certain look on their faces. You know the one."

"Totally," Annie agreed. "My parents do that all the time."

"And we don't think your idea is dumb at all," Cassie added. She got up onto her knees. "I guess

I'm next." Shyly she took a photo out of her pocket.

Annie leaned over so she could see it. "*David Silver?*" she asked incredulously. "You're putting a photo of *David Silver* into the hope chest?"

David Silver was a guy in their seventh-grade class at Summerville Middle School. They'd gone to school with him forever. He was nice-looking and smart, but really quiet and shy. Cassie had a huge crush on him.

"I like him," Cassie admitted.

"Yeah, like the whole town of Summerville doesn't know that," Annie snorted. "What does David Silver have to do with our hope chest?"

"Well, someday I'm going to . . . I'm going to marry him," Cassie said.

"Get out of here," Annie guffawed.

"Annie, be nice," Breezy scolded. "We said we could put anything we wanted into the hope chest."

"Yeah, but it was supposed to be something *important*," Annie pointed out, blowing a huge bubble with her bubble gum. "Not David Silver."

"He's important to me," Cassie said, jutting out her chin, "even if he never talks to me."

"He's shy," Breezy said.

Cassie nodded. "I know. But maybe someday . . ." Her voice trailed off.

"Maybe," Breezy agreed.

"Oh, I almost forgot," Cassie said, reaching into her pocket again. "There's more. I wrote a short story about him." She took a folded-up piece of notebook paper out of her pocket and read her very short short story, which was more like a fairy tale.

". . . and Prince David and Princess Cassie lived happily ever after," she concluded.

"*Prince* David?" Annie repeated dubiously. "*Princess* Cassie? David Silver is supposed to be a prince who meets you in the mall while you're trying on shoes, and he whisks you away to his kingdom and you become a princess and get really, really rich?"

"Isn't it great?" Cassie said dreamily.

"It's . . . original," Annie said, laughing.

"Well, I think it's great," Breezy said loyally.

Annie reached for the last of the popcorn and put her already chewed gum on her finger so she could rechew it after she ate. "All I have to say, Cassie, is that you really put the romance in romantic."

"Don't you ever dream about who you're going to marry?" Cassie asked Annie.

"Nope," Annie said. "I'm never getting married. Yuck." She stuck her gum back into her mouth, yanked a Nerf ball out of her back pocket, and started spinning it on one finger like a pro basketball player.

"I dream about it a lot," Cassie admitted. "What my wedding will be like, what my gown will look like . . ."

"Yuck again," Annie said again, bouncing the ball on the tip of her finger.

"You'll change your mind one day," Cassie predicted. She carefully put the short story and the photo of David Silver into the hope chest.

"Doubtful," Annie replied.

"I think we need to say something special before we lock up the hope chest," Cassie suggested.

"You're right," Breezy agreed. She wrapped her hands around the key hanging from her neck. So did the others. "We three best friends, Breezy, Cassie, and Annie," she intoned, "do solemnly swear never to tell any secrets we share in this room — "

"And never to tell the contents of the hope chest," Annie finished.

"Amen," Cassie added.

Breezy reached out for her two friends, so that their hands formed a circle. "We will keep each other's secrets forever, and our circle will never be broken."

They held their joined hands high. "Forever!" they all cried.

They had no way of knowing just how soon their "forever" would be tested. Or which of the three of them would be the one to betray them all.

10

2

"Girls, are you up there?" Breezy's mom called up the attic stairs.

"Yeah, Mom," Breezy called back. She quickly lowered the hope chest's top, and then took the key from around her neck and locked it.

Her mother's head came into view as she climbed the attic stairs.

"Doesn't it look great in here?" Breezy asked her mom. She was pretty sure her mother had been so busy lately with her business that she hadn't seen the attic in its totally finished state.

"Uh-huh," Mrs. Zeeman said, but Breezy could tell her mother wasn't really listening, which was odd for her.

"Hello, Mrs. Zeeman," Cassie said politely. She really liked Breezy's mom, who was much younger than her own mother. Mrs. Zeeman had the same flyaway brown hair as Breezy and a really pretty, round face, and she was always full of energy and surprises.

11

"Hi, Mrs. Z.," Annie said, giving Breezy's mom a quick wave.

Breezy's mom and Annie's mom were best friends. For the past eight years they'd even owned a business together, Perfect Weddings.

Perfect Weddings was designed to help people get married. Couples who were getting married, or parents of the bride or groom, hired Perfect Weddings to plan every detail of the weddings, from the invitations to the honeymoon. The company was very successful and popular in the northern Indianapolis suburbs, and the two moms had even talked of expanding their business to Indianapolis, and then to the rest of Indiana.

As for Cassie's parents, they had already been in their forties when they adopted her as an infant. Now they were in their fifties, and had recently taken early retirement from the Summerville post office. Even though Cassie really loved her parents, sometimes she felt jealous that Breezy's and Annie's parents were so young. Sometimes other kids mistook them for her grandparents, which was really embarrassing.

Recently, though, her parents had done something so fantastic that it pretty much made up for how old they were, and how conservative they were, and anything else they were.

To Cassie's shock and delight, they had decided to open a bridal shop in the new mall in Carmel. Like Cassie, her mother was a great romantic, and she loved the idea of helping brides-to-be pick out their perfect wedding gown. Cassie figured she had the world's greatest after-school and summer job all set and couldn't wait until she was old enough to work there part-time. In fact, even now, she tried to hang out at the shop as much as her mother would let her.

"Did you girls get a snack and do your homework?" Mrs. Zeeman asked them. She was dressed in a business suit with her hair pulled back, but instead of having her usual sunny smile on her face, she looked anxious and stressed.

"We got a snack," Breezy said.

"And we got to have a study hall last period at school because we had a sub, so we didn't have any homework," Annie added.

"Well, we did," Breezy corrected her, as usual being honest to a fault. "But it's not due until — "

"No homework," Annie said adamantly, kicking Breezy so that Breezy's mom couldn't see.

"That's great news," Mrs. Zeeman said.

"I agree, Mrs. Z.," Annie said, grinning. "Homework is the worst."

"Uh-huh," Mrs. Zeeman said, her mind clearly on something else.

Breezy was surprised. Nothing was more serious to her mom than school. Under normal circumstances, she would definitely have followed up on the homework thing. "What's up, Mom?" Breezy asked.

13

"Girls, Paula and I are in a major crisis," Mrs. Zeeman said.

Paula, Mrs. McGee, was Annie's mom. "My mom's idea of a crisis is if they serve Pepsi instead of Coke," Annie said. "Is it one of those?"

"Much bigger than that," Mrs. Zeeman said. "In exactly thirty minutes, the rehearsal dinner for the Laramie wedding will begin. There are eight kids between the ages of two and nine who need to be entertained during the dinner. We hired Shannon Eagleton to watch them all tonight, but Shannon just called to say she broke her ankle playing Frisbee in the park and she's still at the emergency room."

"Wait, are you saying you want us to do it?" Breezy asked, surprised. Shannon Eagleton was a junior in high school and sixteen, and she babysat all the time. Breezy had just started babysitting, and she certainly had never baby-sat for eight kids at once before.

"If you three girls could fill in tonight, you'd be doing us a huge favor," Mrs. Zeeman said. "Paula and I already tried calling all of Shannon's friends, but no one is available!"

Breezy looked over at her friends. "Can you guys do it?"

Annie made a face. "No offense, Breezy, but I hate little kids. You know that."

"Oh, come on," Breezy said. "The moms need help." She and Annie always referred to their mothers as "the moms." And the moms liked it. In fact, even they sometimes referred to themselves as the moms.

"Yeah, yeah," Annie said, sighing. "Well, obviously I don't have to ask my mom." She looked over at Cassie. "How about you?"

"I'll call my parents at the shop and ask," Cassie said. "But my mom will say yes. If it involves a wedding, I'm fine."

Mrs. Zeeman's face broke into a huge grin. "You three are the greatest. I hope you know that."

"Don't say that until after we do the job," Breezy warned. The idea of taking care of so many kids at once made her kind of nervous.

"You'll be fantastic," her mother assured her. "Oh, just one little thing I should mention."

"What's that?" Breezy asked.

"Watch out for the five-year-old boy from Florida. He bites."

"*Bites?*" Cassie echoed.

Mrs. Zeeman nodded. "And the two-year-old seems to be having trouble keeping food down."

"A biter and a barfer?" Annie asked incredulously. "Are you kidding?"

"No, really," Mrs. Zeeman said, distractedly looking at her watch. "We are already so late. Cassie, as soon as you call your mom, we're out of here." She handed a portable phone to Cassie and hurried down the stairs.

"I have a feeling this is not going to be the greatest night of my life," Annie said as Cassie started to dial the number at her parents' bridal shop.

Breezy closed the hope chest and locked it. "Maybe it'll be fun," she ventured.

"Yeah, like a math test." Annie grimaced.

"I like taking care of little kids. They're so cute," Cassie said, and then she spoke into the phone. "Hi, Mom, guess what?"

"Maybe on Planet Cassie they are," Annie said. "In the real world, they're a big pain." She got up, grabbed Breezy's hand, and hauled her to her feet as Cassie started explaining to her mom about the baby-sitting job. "All I can say is, I will remember this day for the rest of my life."

"Because of our secrets in the hope chest," Cassie agreed, nodding.

"Wrong," Annie said. "Because this is the day I, Annie McGee, was dumb enough to volunteer to get bitten and hurled on by eight little rugrats!"

3

Annie stood in the front hallway of the Laramies' house, looked down at her stinky, soiled right sneaker, and made a face. "This is totally disgusting. I told you guys that it was dumb to volunteer to do this thing."

"But it was fun," Cassie called to her as she and Breezy stood in the front doorway of the Laramies' spacious ranch house, waving good-bye to the last set of parents whose kids the three girls had baby-sat.

"This was your concept of *fun*?" Annie asked.

"Mine too, kind of," Breezy agreed. She and Cassie walked back into the house. "And just think of the bride and groom, and how happy they must be."

"Sure," Annie agreed. "They didn't have to deal with eight midget monsters for three hours."

Finally, the rehearsal dinner was over. Mr. and Mrs. Laramie, the parents of the groom, were now back home, in the kitchen doing a little bit of

17

cleaning up, although the phone had rung a couple of times to interrupt them. The girls had just seen off the last of the kids. Soon Mrs. Zeeman and Mrs. McGee would show up to take them home.

"Wasn't that little girl Amy the cutest?" Cassie asked. "I loved braiding her hair."

"Yeah, you braided her hair while Scotty let fly on my new sneakers," Annie said, dabbing at her right shoe with an old rag, trying to wipe off the barf spot.

"He hardly hit it," Breezy said, trying to make her friend feel better. "You can barely see anything."

"But you sure can smell it," Annie said. "And how about his cousin, Brett the Biter? The kid took a hunk out of my leg!" She lifted the bottom of her jeans and then pulled down her white athletic sock. Sure enough, there was a telltale round mark where the five-year-old from Florida had proved his nickname correct.

"At least he didn't break the skin," Breezy said as the three girls headed into the family room to relax until their moms showed up.

"Good thing," Annie groused. "Or we'd be making a trip to the hospital now."

"And then to the animal shelter, to bring in the Biter," Breezy joked, which cracked up all three of them.

"I bet you never bit your baby-sitter," Annie said to Breezy.

"My best baby-sitter was Crystal Anders," Breezy recalled. "She was so nice — she taught me how to bake the best chocolate chip cookies. She graduated from high school and left town a long time ago, but her mother's still here, if you want to call and ask her."

"Breezy, I was *joking*," Annie said, rolling her eyes. "I knew you when you were a kid, remember? The only thing you bit into was junk food."

Mr. Laramie stuck his head into the family room. "Hey, I just got another phone call about you girls. You three are getting absolutely great reviews," he said happily.

"What do you mean?" Cassie asked.

"What I mean is that the phone has already rung twice from parents whose kids were here," he explained. "They said their kids loved you. They can't stop talking about you."

"Even Brett the Biter?" Annie asked dubiously. "Mr. Teeth himself?"

Mr. Laramie smiled at her. "His parents haven't called yet. If it's any consolation, Annie, look." He bent down and lifted up his own trouser leg.

Sure enough, there was a red mark there suspiciously like the one Brett had left on Annie's calf.

"The things we do for family," he said with a laugh as he rubbed the red spot gingerly. "He's nailed me twice in two days. Good thing the wedding is tomorrow."

Just then Mrs. Zeeman and Mrs. McGee hurried into the family room with Mrs. Laramie.

"Hi, Bill," Mrs. Zeeman said to Mr. Laramie, who waved and grinned at them.

"We're sooooo sorry," Mrs. McGee said, her voice stressed out.

"About what?" Mr. Laramie asked.

"We didn't have time to call and check on how the girls were doing with the kids," Mrs. Zeeman admitted.

"Not to worry," Mr. Laramie said. "From what I hear through the grapevine — and the telephone — your girls did just fine."

"Little Amy's mom told me she's never heard Amy go on and on about how much she loved a sitter before," Mrs. Laramie said, beaming at the three girls. The phone rang again.

"I'll get it," Mr. Laramie said, hurrying toward the kitchen. "I bet it's another glowing report about the kids."

"Sounds like you girls were a hit," Mrs. Zeeman said, grinning.

"Did anything go wrong?" Annie's mom asked. She tended to stress out as much as Breezy's mom took things in stride.

"Not a thing," Breezy assured her.

"Yeah, it was keen," Annie said under her breath, rubbing the bite mark on her calf. "Super."

"It really was!" Cassie agreed, too enthusiastic

to catch Annie's sarcasm. From her point of view, it really had gone great. She had loved all the kids, and all the kids had loved her. She was the only one who had been able to get Brett the Biter to stop biting. In fact, all the kids had flocked around her. She just had a way with them.

"I thought it went really well," Breezy said, nodding. At first she had felt totally overwhelmed by the job. After all, none of the kids they were taking care of even knew them. But after the first half hour, when Cassie was reading the older kids a story and Annie was playing duck-duck-goose with the little kids, Breezy started to relax. The kids actually hadn't been too much work, and she knew that they had helped her mom out in a big way, which made her feel really good.

Mrs. Zeeman looked over at Annie. "Hey, Miss Annie," she said playfully, "I don't hear you saying how great it was."

"Are you kidding? I'm ready to marry Brett the Biter," Annie replied.

"You really hated it, huh?" her mom asked.

"Nah, it was okay," Annie said quickly. She didn't want her mom to feel bad. And actually, other than the Biter and the barfer, it really had been . . . well, *almost* fun.

"Well, Paula," Mrs. Zeeman said, "I suppose it's time for us to settle up."

Settle up?

Annie looked at Cassie who looked at Breezy

who looked at Annie. Settle up? As in . . . get *paid*?

"Do you mean . . ." Breezy began. But then she wasn't sure if she should say "get paid," because maybe that wasn't what her mom meant at all.

Annie wasn't nearly so shy. "You mean you're *paying* us?" she asked incredulously.

"Of course," her mother said. "You certainly earned it."

"But you don't have to do that," Breezy said. "We didn't do this for money. We did it to help you out."

Cassie nodded. "That's right, Mrs. Zeeman. Anything we can do to help a wedding . . . well, anything that I can do, I mean, I'm happy to do for free."

"Don't listen to them," Annie said quickly. "I mean, of course we weren't *planning* on getting paid, but if you really want to pay us, how could we turn you down?"

Mrs. Zeeman laughed. "Right." She turned to her daughter. "What you and Cassie said is really sweet, honey, but you earned the money. Besides, those sentiments won't take you all to the mall on Sunday."

"Good point," Cassie said, nodding.

Annie's mom unzipped her purse. "We'll pay in cash, right, Stephanie?"

"Right, Paula," Mrs. Zeeman said.

"But Mom — "

Breezy's mom cut off her daughter's sentence with a wave of a hand that Breezy knew meant that there was to be no further discussion, because the issue was settled.

The girls couldn't believe it. And they really couldn't believe it when Mrs. McGee handed each of them a twenty-dollar bill.

"Did you, uh . . . want change?" Annie asked.

"No," her mother said.

"Twenty dollars!" Cassie said, staring at the bill in the palm of her hand.

"For each of us," Annie repeated, visualizing the new hockey sticks in the sporting goods store that she wanted for next year's season. "Hey, Mom?"

"Yes?" Annie's mother responded.

"Can you take me shopping tomorrow?" Annie gave her mother her toothiest grin.

"When this wedding madness is over," Mrs. McGee said.

"Awww . . ." Annie replied, but she was smiling.

"Thanks, Mom!" Breezy said to her own mother. "This is so great!"

Annie and Cassie chimed in with another round of thank-yous, too.

"You girls are welcome," Mrs. Zeeman said. She gave her daughter a fond look and brushed Breezy's hair off her face. "My little girl is growing up."

Breezy quickly shook her hair back in place. "Twenty dollars just for baby-sitting. Amazing!"

Mrs. Zeeman laughed. "Hey, I think we got off cheap!"

"I do, too," Mrs. McGee agreed, rezipping her purse.

"But you won't even up my allowance from last year," Annie pointed out.

"That's different," her mother said. "That's family, this is business." She looped the strap of her purse over her shoulder. "Here's how I look at it. If we were living in New York City, we'd owe each of you girls forty bucks!"

The girls just looked at each other. Forty bucks? For baby-sitting?

"I just made a decision," Annie announced.

"What?" Cassie asked.

Annie grinned and threw her arms out. "I am *definitely* moving to New York!"

4

Breezy stood for a moment and admired her twenty-dollar bill from the baby-sitting venture, which she had pinned jauntily to the mannequin in the attic clubhouse. Breezy's mind was working overtime. *If my plan works*, she thought, *there could be more twenty-dollar bills up there. A lot more.*

It was a few days later — the Laramie wedding had gone off without a hitch — and Annie and Cassie were supposed to come over and hang out after school, and then work together on a group report for social studies.

But for once, Breezy wasn't thinking about homework. The night before, an incredible idea had come into her head, and she was about to share it with her friends.

Now, if only they thought her idea was as great as she thought it was, everything would be super. But Breezy was nervous. And when she got nervous, she ate. She stuck her hand into the large bag of M&Ms she'd brought up from the kitchen.

"M&Ms!" Annie said as she flew up the stairs two at a time and saw Breezy. "My fave!" She threw her books on the floor, plopped herself down, and reached into the bag of candy. "I beat Cassie here, huh?" she asked, her mouth full.

"No, you didn't," Cassie said, bounding up behind her. "Hey, how did you guys do on that math test?"

Annie groaned and reached for more M&Ms. "Why does Mr. Butler give us those stupid pop quizzes?"

"To see if we really studied," Breezy explained.

"Well, guess who didn't study," Annie admitted. "What does math have to do with real life, anyway?"

"You have to know math if you're going to fly around the world," Breezy said. "All those instruments — "

"Everything is computerized," Annie said, waving her off. She did a handstand and walked across the floor on her hands. "I suppose you two want to work on that dumb social studies project." She stopped in front of a chalkboard on an easel, which hadn't been in the attic before, and regarded it from her upside-down position. "What is this?"

"That's what I was about to tell you guys," Breezy said nervously.

"Hey, Breezy, how come you pinned your

money to the mannequin?" Cassie asked.

"Actually, I was about to answer both of those questions." Breezy took a deep breath. She felt really nervous. "Last night, just before I fell asleep, I had this great idea."

Annie did a cartwheel and sat down next to Breezy again. She reached for more M&Ms and held the bag out to Cassie.

Cassie was the only girl they knew who didn't like junk food. Instead of taking an M&M, she opened her backpack and took out a box of sugar-free, additive-free mints from the health food store and popped one into her mouth.

"How can you eat that junk?" Annie asked, making a face.

"It's very healthy," Cassie said. "It's natural."

"So is mud, but that doesn't mean I want to eat it," Annie replied. She turned back to Breezy. "So, what's this big idea you had?"

Breezy had planned exactly how she was going to present her brainstorm to her friends, had carefully chosen her sentences and marshaled her arguments. She'd even rehearsed it in front of the bathroom mirror right after she'd come home from school.

But now, with Annie and Cassie staring at her, all her careful planning went out the window.

"We should go into business," Breezy said very quickly.

"What?" Cassie asked, confused.

"Not just any business," Breezy hurried on. "What I meant was that we should go into the wedding business. Not like the moms, but doing all the kid stuff for weddings. You know, like we did with the Laramies. There're all kinds of other things that involve kids and weddings. And other stuff we can do to help out. And we can get paid for doing it."

Cassie and Annie didn't say a word. Breezy was sure they hated her idea.

"You know," Cassie finally said, "that is a really brilliant idea."

"It is?" Breezy asked hopefully.

"Just think," Cassie went on, "we'd be around weddings all the time. That would be so great!"

Breezy knew she was halfway home. Cassie was in the bag. She turned to Annie.

"We'd get paid," she reminded her friend. "A lot!"

"Paid a lot is good," Annie allowed. "But I still hate little kids."

"What if adults said that about you when you were a little kid?" Cassie asked her. "No one would have taken care of you! Besides, they don't all bite, you know."

"I'll bet something like fifty percent of them do," Annie decided. "And the rest throw up. On me."

"What if . . . what if I were to guarantee you'd

28

never have to deal with the biters and the barfers?" Breezy asked, thinking fast.

Annie cocked her head at Breezy. "How are you going to do that?"

"Well, if we ever get any kids like that, I'll take care of them."

"Or I will," Cassie added, and Breezy smiled at her gratefully.

Annie gave Breezy a dubious look. "You swear it?"

"On my honor," Breezy said.

"Mine too," Cassie chimed in.

Annie thought another minute. "Okay. Well, then . . . I'm in."

Breezy and Cassie screamed with excitement.

"You're the best, Annie!" Breezy said happily.

"I'm only doing it for the money," Annie said honestly, hugging her knees to her chest. "I need new hockey sticks for youth league in the fall. And a new helmet, and new skates."

"This is going to be so fantastic!" Cassie cried. "Our own business!"

"You guys, we need a name for our business." Breezy walked over to the erasable board and uncapped the felt-tipped marker. "Any suggestions?"

"Ummmm . . . The Wedding Friends?" Cassie asked.

Annie made a face. "Lame-o."

"How about Bridal Buddies?" Breezy tried.

"Ugh," all three of them said at once.

"Okay, how about Young Weddings, then?" Breezy suggested. She'd actually been so worried about convincing Annie and Cassie to join in on the new business that she hadn't thought much about a name for it.

"Young Weddings sounds like a soap opera your sister would watch," Annie said, laughing. She knew that Breezy's sister, Liza, was a big fan of *Days of Our Lives*.

"You're right," Breezy said. "It does."

"And it also sounds like we'll only work on a wedding if the couple getting married is young," Cassie pointed out.

Annie lay on her back and put her hands under her head. "Maybe it should be something like 'Breezy, Cassie, and Annie,'" she mused, reaching for her baseball cap. She threw it toward the ceiling and caught it. "You know, use our names."

"But no one would know what kind of business it was," Breezy pointed out.

"Annie, Breezy, Cassie," Cassie said slowly. "Hey, do you realize that's ABC?"

"That's it!" Breezy shouted.

"What's it?" Annie asked, sitting up. She popped her baseball cap onto her head.

"That's the name," Breezy said.

"ABC?" Cassie asked. "I don't get it."

Annie laughed. "Hey, remember when we were

30

little and ABC stood for already-been-chewed gum?"

"That was then, this is now," Breezy said. She wrote ABC WEDDINGS on the board, in big block letters.

"Hey, that's good," Cassie said.

"Plus my name is first!" Annie added impishly.

"It's alphabetical," Breezy pointed out.

"Breezer, lighten up," Annie said. "I *know* that."

"I am so excited, I can't stand it," Cassie said. "Our own business, ABC Weddings!"

"You guys really promise that if we get any biters you're taking them?" Annie asked again.

"We already promised we would," Breezy told her.

Annie got up. "Then we're in business. ABC Weddings it is."

"What if we make hundreds of dollars?" Cassie asked breathlessly. "Or thousands, even?"

"Then I get the best ice hockey equipment any girl ever had," Annie said. She grinned at Breezy. "Breezer, this was about the greatest idea you ever had, other than hanging out with me, of course."

"Thanks," Breezy said. She felt really happy. After all, Annie didn't hand out a compliment unless she really, really meant it.

"You know what we need to do now?" Annie asked her friends.

"Plan how we're going to advertise ABC Weddings?" Breezy guessed.

"Please," Annie scoffed. "How can I do that on an empty stomach? The three owners of ABC Weddings need to go raid the refrigerator!"

"I'm kind of trying to cut down on junk food," Breezy said.

"You?" Annie asked incredulously. "You love junk food. You live for junk food."

"I think it's great if you're going to try to eat healthier," Cassie said. "I have an organic energy bar in my backpack — "

"Yuck! Blech! Gag me!" Annie yelled. "I'm talking Doritos with dip!"

"That sounds a lot better than an energy bar," Breezy admitted. "Maybe I'll just eat a few less Doritos."

"Now you're talking," Annie agreed, scrambling to her feet.

"Okay, junk food now, work later. Deal?" Breezy asked.

"Last one downstairs has to load the dishwasher!" Annie called out.

Even as she said it, she was halfway down the stairs.

5

It was after school several days later, and Annie and Cassie were on their way over to Breezy's house. Annie was depressed.

"I got a C- on that stupid pop quiz in math today," Annie said as they walked up to the Zeemans' front porch. "My parents are going to be so ticked off if I get a C in math on my report card." She opened the front door — as usual it wasn't locked.

"I could help you study, if you want," Cassie offered.

They headed for the stairs that led to the attic. "If studying is so good for you, why is it so boring, that's what I want to know," Annie said.

"My mom would say you need an attitude adjustment," Cassie said as they trudged up the stairs.

"Don't you just hate it when parents say stuff like that? I really hate it. You know what else I really hate?"

"What?" Cassie asked patiently.

"Finding out that we're big failures."

Breezy, who was already up in the attic, heard what Annie had said. "That is not true," she insisted.

"Is too." Annie plopped down on a giant corduroy-covered pillow. "We spent one entire week putting up flyers about ABC Weddings all over town. The phone has not rung once. All we have to show for it is blisters on our feet."

She looked at the pile of posters they had made and photocopied at the local Kinko's.

ABC WEDDINGS!
Three great girls will help you
with all the wedding stuff you
don't want to do, have time to do,
or didn't think to do. No job is too
small! Our parents own Perfect
Weddings, Inc. and the mall Bridal
Shoppe, so we know our stuff!
A: Always on time.
B: Baby-sitting. We also
    care for pets and plants!
C: Can Do. That's our
    attitude!
— ABC WEDDINGS. Annie McGee,
Breezy Zeeman, and Cassie Pearson.
References available. Satisfaction guaranteed!

The girls had even been smart enough to make the posters half the size of a standard sheet of paper, so they could get double use out of a single page. And the poster listed in big numbers the Perfect Weddings phone number in addition to Breezy's home phone, since the moms had agreed to refer any calls for them over to ABC Weddings.

"You really need to think more positively," Cassie said, dropping her backpack next to Annie's.

"I'm not in a very positive mood," Annie said. "Our fantastic business idea is a total failure."

"We had one call," Cassie pointed out.

"Cassie, it was a wrong number," Annie reminded her. "The person wanted to order a pizza."

"Okay, I admit we haven't been very successful so far," Breezy said. "But maybe we haven't given it enough time yet." She reached into a giant bag of pretzels.

"Face it, it was a crummy idea," Annie said. "No one is going to hire us to help with a wedding."

"The moms did," Breezy pointed out.

"Breeze, they're the moms," Annie said. "And even they wouldn't have hired us if they hadn't been desperate at the very last minute."

Cassie sighed. "I suppose you're right. It sure would have been fun, though, if it had worked."

"I was already planning how I was going to spend all the money I made," Annie said.

Breezy stared accusingly at the phone her parents had agreed she could put in the attic to take calls about ABC Weddings. It was the same number as the family phone, but at least in the attic she could take calls in private.

Except that there were no calls to take.

"You guys, I don't think we should just give up." Breezy chomped down hard on another pretzel. "We'll just have to figure out a way to get some publicity for ABC Weddings."

"Or we could forget about the whole thing. It'll probably interfere with baseball practice, anyway," Annie said. She turned to Breezy. "Hey, by the way, what time is the party tomorrow night? Because I've got a game that starts at four. I'm pitching."

Annie was one of two girls who had been selected for the Summerville Sluggers baseball team, a travel team for boys and girls in seventh and eighth grades. At tryouts, Annie, who had a wicked curveball, had struck out all three batters she had faced, and then tripled off the left field fence in her at bat.

"The party starts at eight," Breezy said, "so you're fine."

"So, what's the occasion for this thing, anyway?" Annie asked. "My mom is so excited that she's running around the house like a crazy lady. I asked her what the big deal was, but all she said was that your parents were giving this big bash for grown-ups and for kids, and if I didn't wear a dress she would trade me in for a new daughter."

Breezy shrugged. "To tell you the truth, I don't know. They just decided they wanted to give a big party."

"Maybe it's to celebrate that school's almost out for the summer," Cassie guessed.

"Or Liza's graduation from college," Annie put in.

Breezy shook her head no. "My grandmother is treating us all to another trip to Florida in honor of Liza's graduation, so it can't be that."

"I think it is so romantic that Liza is dating Annie's brother," Cassie said, hugging a pillow to her chest.

"Romantic to you, maybe. I think Greg is a pain in the butt," Annie said. "I have no idea in the world what Liza sees in him."

"Well, he's cute," Cassie began, "and really nice. And he's smart, and he's — "

"My yucky brother," Annie concluded.

Cassie grabbed Breezy's hands. "Listen, I hope you don't mind if I change the subject, but . . . is it really true that David Silver will be at the party?"

Breezy nodded. "His parents are really good friends with my parents. My mom said the whole family is coming."

Cassie put her hand over her mouth. "What if he actually asks me to dance?"

"Then . . . you dance," Annie suggested.

"Oh, my gosh, I would die," Cassie said, throwing herself back onto the rug. She stared up at the ceiling, as if a movie about her and David were unfolding from above. "He'd put his hand on my back, and then he'd take my hand in his, and then — "

"He'd step on your foot and you'd fall over in front of everyone and be totally embarrassed," Annie finished. She reached for the pretzels.

Breezy nudged her foot into Annie to make her stop teasing Cassie. "Maybe he *will* ask you to dance, Cassie," she said. "You want me to tell him you like him?"

"No!" Cassie said quickly, sitting up.

"Everyone already knows you like him," Annie groaned.

"Maybe," Cassie admitted. "But you can't actually tell him! You have to promise!"

"We promise," Breezy said. "Hey, I just thought of something. Maybe if we bring a whole lot of flyers about ABC Weddings to the party, we'll drum up some business."

"That's a good idea, actually," Annie agreed. "Everyone at the party already knows us, so it's not like we have to convince them that we're mature enough. Of course, if my parents find out I got another C– on a math quiz, I may be under house arrest."

"Tomorrow night is going to be so fabulous," Cassie predicted. "I'll dance with David, he'll fall madly in love with me, we'll get a whole bunch of jobs for ABC Weddings — "

"And I know exactly who you'll hire to work on your wedding," Annie said innocently.

"Who?" Cassie asked.

Annie grinned. "Us!"

6

"**D**o I look okay?" Cassie asked Breezy anxiously as she walked into the front hall of the Zeemans' house the next night. Her parents had entered ahead of her and were already having an animated discussion with Breezy's parents.

"You look so cute," Breezy assured her.

"Thanks," Cassie said. "I got so nervous, I didn't know what to wear."

Cassie had on a short pink sleeveless dress and matching pink sandals.

Breezy peered closer at her friend's face. "Do you have on makeup?"

Cassie nodded. "I begged. My mother finally gave in. She only let me wear pale lipstick and no-color mascara, but it's better than nothing." She moved a little closer to Breezy. "I snuck a little blush, too. Does it look okay?"

"Fantastic," Breezy said, even though she had never worn makeup and didn't plan to anytime soon. "You look older."

"Really?" Cassie asked. "That's great! You look so pretty, Breezy."

Breezy looked down at her long flowered skirt and matching short-sleeved sweater. "My mom bought me this for tonight."

"It's darling, honest," Cassie told her. Her eyes began to wander around the hallway, as if she was trying to see past the crowds of people into the family room. "Is you-know-who here?" she whispered to Breezy.

"He's in the family room with his best friend, Ben. They brought a Game Boy. The last time I saw them Annie was beating the pants off of them at Tetris."

Cassie sighed. "I wish I could talk to those guys as easily as Annie does."

"It's easier for her 'cause she doesn't care about them," Breezy confided. "Maybe if you pretended you didn't care, then — "

"Hey, you guys!" Annie called, hurrying over to them. She hugged Cassie, then peered at her face. "Makeup?"

Cassie nodded.

"Gross," Annie said. "Not for you, though," she added hastily. She looked down at herself. "Can you even deal with this dress my mother made me wear?"

Annie's dress was pale blue, with sheer sleeves, and her hair fell in soft red curls around her face. Since Annie lived in baggy clothes (mostly to hide the fact that she already had a figure) and baseball caps, it was very unusual to see her minus her baseball cap and dressed up in feminine clothes that actually fit.

"I think you look beautiful," Cassie said honestly. Suddenly she felt horribly insecure. After all, Annie looked so cute now that she was out of her usual scruffy clothes. And it was so easy for Annie to talk to guys.

Even David Silver.

And what guy wouldn't like a girl who could talk to him better than a girl who was too shy to open her mouth?

"You should dress like that more often," Cassie added.

"Ugh," Annie said, looking down at herself. "This is so not me." She nudged Cassie in the ribs with her elbow. "In case you're wondering, the love of your life is out on the patio playing Hacky Sack with Ben Newman and some other guys."

"Shhhh!" Cassie said, her face reddening.

Annie looked around. "No one heard me."

"Hey, I've got an idea," Breezy said. "How about if we go out there and leave the sliding glass doors into the family room open? Maybe that way he'll hear the music in the family room and ask you to dance, Cassie."

"I just don't want to look too obvious," Cassie said nervously.

"You won't," Breezy assured her. "Come on."

As they made their way through the crowded party, Breezy explained to her friends that she had already passed out flyers about ABC to every adult there.

"So what kind of reaction did you get?" Annie asked as she dodged around two little kids playing tag.

"Hard to say," Breezy admitted. "You know how adults are. They say all the right things, but you usually can't tell how they really feel."

"Or if they'll ever actually hire you and pay you actual money," Annie said, nodding.

Just as they were about to step through the sliding glass doors onto the patio, Cassie grabbed her friends and pulled them close. "You guys, do I have lipstick or gunk on my teeth?" She bared her teeth at them so they could check.

"No lipstick, no gunk," Annie assured her, peering into her mouth.

The girls stepped out onto the patio and left the door open behind them. David and his best friend, Ben Newman, were in a serious game of Hacky Sack with two high-school guys. Cassie did her best to try to look casual. She noticed how Annie was standing and tried to copy her.

"Hey, man, you cheated!" Ben cried. "You can't use your hands!"

"I didn't," the older guy insisted. "Why would I bother to cheat with two little twerps like you?"

His friend smirked and nodded.

David shook his head ruefully. "I saw you hit the sack with your hand, too. Why don't you just admit it?"

"So . . . " Breezy began. "Are you guys having fun?"

"Sure," David said. "Except for those guys."

For a long moment no one could think of anything to say. Inside in the family room, the music changed to the Spice Girls.

"The Spice Girls are great," Breezy said, trying to make conversation. She turned to Cassie. "You like them, don't you?"

"Who are they?" Cassie asked blankly.

"Duh," Annie replied. "Earth to Cassie. The Spice Girls?"

Cassie blushed. "Oh. Right. I knew that."

"The Spice Girls are so lame," Annie went on, leaning against the house. "They only got picked to be in the band because they're cute, not because they're good musicians."

"Well, they're good to dance to," Breezy said, pleased with her own brilliance in turning the conversation to dancing. "Don't you think so, David?"

David shrugged. "They're okay."

"Wow, look at all those people inside dancing," Breezy added. She saw her sister, Liza, dance by in the arms of Annie's brother, Greg. Then she turned back to David. "You know, Cassie is a really, really good dancer."

44

Cassie's gold skin blushed the color of over-ripe tomatoes. David wouldn't even make eye contact with her.

"So . . . wow, it would really be fun to dance," Breezy said pointedly.

"You want to dance?" Ben asked her.

Breezy felt like screaming in frustration. She had meant that it would be fun for *David* to ask *Cassie* to dance.

"Hey, how about if we all go in and dance together?" Annie suggested. Breezy could have kissed her. Cassie was still too embarrassed to even look up.

"I have to go . . . do something," David mumbled, and he shuffled off with his hands in his pockets.

Ben looked really uncomfortable to be left with the three girls without his friend. "Oh, yeah, well, I guess I do, too," he said quickly, and hurried after David.

"He *hates* me," Cassie cried, putting her head in her hands.

"He does not," Annie insisted. "He's just really shy. Besides, you turn into this idiot every time you're around him. Can't you just be yourself?"

"You guys, what if — " Breezy began, but she was interrupted by her mom's loud voice, asking everyone to come into the family room for a special announcement.

Everyone at the party crowded into the large

family room, waiting to hear what the big news was. Breezy's mom was hugging Annie's mom, while their husbands laughed together. Behind them stood Liza and Greg, hand in hand.

Annie and Breezy made eye contact, to see if the other one knew what was up, but they both just shrugged.

Mrs. Zeeman looked out at the happy, expectant faces of all her friends, and raised her voice once again.

"Everyone, this is a very, very special day for our family and for the McGee family. As you know, our daughter, Liza, and Paula and Al's son, Greg, have been sweethearts since middle school."

"He threw a spitwad at me in the cafeteria!" Liza called out. Everyone laughed. Greg put his arm around her waist and kissed her cheek.

"Hopefully, they've grown up a little since then, since they're both about to graduate from college," Mrs. McGee added.

"Hopefully," Mrs. Zeeman agreed. Her husband came up next to her and took her hand. She smiled at him, then turned back to the crowd. "Tonight, in front of our families and our friends, we are happy to announce the engagement of our daughter, Ms. Liza Anne Zeeman, to Mr. Gregory Michael McGee!"

Everyone began to applaud, talking, exclaiming, and laughing all at once.

46

Annie and Breezy just stared at each other, openmouthed.

"You two really didn't know?" Cassie asked them.

"Not a clue!" Annie said.

"I can't believe they kept this a secret," Breezy said. "Oh, wow, Annie — we're going to be related!"

They screamed and hugged each other hard.

Once again, Cassie felt left out. But she forced herself to shake off the feeling. After all, she didn't have an older brother or sister who could get engaged to someone. She decided to do what she was always telling Annie to do — think positively.

"This is the most romantic thing I have ever heard in my life," Cassie rhapsodized. "Hey, Breezy, remember when you told us you found a poem Greg had written to Liza way back when they were both thirteen, saying that he was going to marry her someday? And now it's really happening!"

"It's so terrific," Breezy said. "I love Greg."

"Well, I love Liza, so we're even," Annie said, laughing. "Hey, Breezer, we're going to be sisters!"

They hugged again, overcome with happiness. "We should go congratulate them, don't you think?" Breezy asked.

"We should congratulate my brother," Annie

said. "He's getting the sweet end of the deal. Come with us, Cassie."

Cassie hugged herself and got a dreamy look on her face. "Someday it's going to be David and me announcing our engagement. And we'll tell everyone how we fell in love when we were only thirteen, just like Liza and Greg."

"Uh, Cassie?" Annie asked. "There's just one little problem."

"What?"

Annie got a mischievous look on her face. "It would be a really good idea to get David Silver to have an actual conversation with you *before* you start planning your wedding!"

7

"It is so great that the moms hired ABC Weddings to work on your wedding, Liza," Cassie told Breezy's older sister.

"I think so, too," Liza said, smiling at Cassie in the rearview mirror. It was a few days later, school was finally out for the summer, and they were in Liza's car, on the way to the roller rink, where Liza was meeting up with Greg. She had agreed to take Breezy, Cassie, and Annie along with her.

Liza was always doing nice things like that. That was one of the reasons Cassie liked her so much. Liza was also really pretty, with her mom's great smile, and best of all, she was a truly good person. So was her fiancé, Greg, for that matter. For example, Liza and Greg did volunteer work together in the pediatric ward at Summerville Hospital, where they regularly dressed up as clowns to entertain the sick little kids who were patients. Liza and Greg had exactly the kind of relationship Cassie wanted for herself one day. With David Silver, of course.

"Since the flyers for ABC Weddings got us zero business, it's a good thing there's a wedding in the family, or we'd be out of business," Annie pointed out.

"We had another call," Cassie said. "It's not going that badly."

This was true. The flyer had prompted another call, and this one was actually about a wedding, and not someone dialing a wrong number for a pizzeria. But it was a couple who wanted the girls to work on a wedding in the little village of Fairmount, which was to the north of Indianapolis. The wedding was scheduled for the same day as Greg and Liza's, and the girls had no way to get back and forth to Fairmount anyway.

So the girls had had to turn the job down.

"I don't know how you can plan your wedding so fast," Cassie told Liza. "I read in *Brides* magazine that you're supposed to start planning a year ahead of time, at least."

Liza laughed. "You read *Brides* magazine?"

Cassie blushed. "I like to look at the clothes."

"She's been reading it since she was ten," Annie said. "Cassie is spending a lot more than a year on planning her wedding!"

"Well, I won't have that luxury," Liza said. "Greg and I don't want to live together until we're married. And since we're both going to grad school in Bloomington in the fall, it didn't make a lot of sense to wait very long."

Cassie leaned as far forward as her seat belt would allow. "So, tell us everything," she begged Liza. "How big is the wedding going to be? What's your dress going to look like? There are some beautiful dresses at my parents' bridal boutique, and — "

"Slow down!" Liza exclaimed as she stopped at a red light. "We're only just starting to plan things. And we have a lot to plan very quickly! It's kind of overwhelming, frankly."

"So maybe you should wait until Christmastime or something," Cassie suggested.

Liza shook her head no as the light changed. "I can't see planning my wedding during my first semester of grad school."

"Well, what kind of wedding do you want?" Breezy asked her sister.

Liza sighed, and a wistful look came over her face. "Oh, you know, a perfect fairy-tale wedding would be kind of nice."

"Then that's what you should have!" Cassie cried with excitement. "Oh, I can just see the whole thing now. . . . "

"I can, too," Liza agreed, turning into the parking lot of the roller rink. "And the moms are in total agreement. The problem is, Greg wants a really small, simple wedding."

"But that's crazy," Cassie protested.

51

"I don't think so," Annie said. "You know I think my big brother is a moron, but frankly, if I ever get married, which I doubt, I'll want a small, simple wedding, too."

"But what fun is that?" Cassie asked.

"That's what I say," Liza said, parking the car. "Greg has other ideas, though. So far we can't seem to agree on anything about the wedding at all." She looked down thoughtfully at her engagement ring. "We even . . . well, we had a fight about it. Don't tell Mom," she added hastily, looking at Breezy.

"I won't," Breezy promised. She felt honored that her big sister would confide something like that to her and her friends. In the past, Liza had treated her like she was still a little kid.

"I didn't think you and Greg ever fought," Annie said.

"We don't, that's what's so terrible about it." Liza twisted her engagement ring around her finger. "I mean, we even fought over the guest list."

"Fought about it how?" Breezy asked.

"Greg wanted me to keep the list down to thirty or forty people from our side. I have more sorority sisters than that!"

"So what did the two of you decide?" Breezy asked.

"We agreed to compromise," Liza said.

Breezy nodded. "That sounds like the right

thing to do. After all, it's his wedding, too."

"But it isn't the same thing," Cassie insisted. "Everyone knows that brides care more about weddings than grooms. This is going to be the most important day of Liza's life. She should have exactly what she wants."

"Who says brides care more?" Annie asked.

"Well, they just do, that's all," Cassie said. "Your brother should be more understanding."

"Cassie — " Breezy began.

"Hey, maybe Breezy's sister needs to be more understanding, ever think of that?"

"Annie — " Breezy said, trying again.

"But if he truly loves her, why wouldn't he want her to have the wedding of her dreams?" Cassie asked Annie.

"If Liza doesn't want to consider his feelings, then maybe she should marry herself!" Annie stormed.

"You guys, stop!" Breezy managed.

Liza smiled. "Gee, the two of you sound a lot like Greg and me."

"They didn't mean anything by it," Breezy told her sister. "I'm sure you and Greg will work it out."

"Right," Cassie agreed. "True love always works out."

"It does not," Annie said, peering out the car window. "Oh, look, there's Greg."

"He's so handsome," Cassie told Liza. "And so

nice and smart and well . . . just everything. You're so lucky."

She watched as Greg walked into the roller rink with his best friend, Pete. Greg was medium height, with short dark blond hair and great blue eyes.

"As long as we're not fighting, I agree with you," Liza said, smiling. She turned back to the younger girls. "Hey, I'd really appreciate it if this was our secret, okay?"

"We would never breathe a word," Cassie said solemnly.

"Besides, like I said, you and Greg will definitely work it all out," Breezy assured her sister.

Liza gave Breezy a quick hug. "You're the greatest, Breeze."

The girls walked into the roller rink and quickly rented skates.

Cassie motioned her friends over to her. "Listen, we should stay far away from Liza and Greg so they can be alone and make up."

"Alone?" Annie asked pointedly, as she looked around at the many dozens of people in the roller rink.

"You know what I mean," Cassie said. "I just want to help along the course of true love."

"Can we just forget about my dumb brother for a little while and skate?" Annie asked.

She sat down on the nearest bench and

changed into her skates. So did Breezy and Cassie.

Annie was the first one out on the floor. She was picking up speed and zooming around little kids before Cassie and Breezy even began to skate.

This was one sport, however, where Cassie truly excelled. She didn't skate as fast as Annie, and she certainly wasn't a daredevil on wheels like Annie, but she could do some jumps and spins that Annie tried over and over to do and never could.

The music changed to something fast as Cassie got ready for her first jump. She twirled in the air and landed perfectly.

"Wow, how did you do that?" a little girl, very wobbly on her skates, asked.

"I practiced," Cassie told her, slowing down so she wouldn't skate away from the little girl. "You can do it, too, if you practice."

"You look just like those ice skaters on TV," the little girl said, her voice full of awe. "Well, except that they have ice skates and you have roller skates. I just learned to skate."

The little girl lurched forward unsteadily, and Cassie put out her hand to help the girl balance. "You're doing a great job," Cassie told her warmly.

The little girl's face lit up. "Thanks! That's my

dad over there." She pointed to a man sitting on a bench, sipping a cold drink. Her dad waved her to come over to him. "I have to go now," the little girl said. "See you."

"See you," Cassie said, and watched the little girl skate slowly, carefully toward her father.

"Who was that?" Breezy asked, skating over to her.

"I don't know. I just met her," Cassie said, still watching the girl skating over to her dad.

Annie skated over to them, whirled around them, then skated backward. "Skate with me, you guys!"

Breezy and Cassie began to skate with Annie. They had gone around the rink twice when Cassie gasped.

"What is it?" Breezy asked her, alarmed.

"Over there," Cassie said, pointing. Her friends turned to look at Liza and Greg. "Don't make it so obvious that we're looking at them!"

It was clear from all the way across the roller rink that Liza and Greg were arguing, and they were much too involved to notice who might or might not be staring at them. Although the girls couldn't hear a word Liza and Greg were saying, it was very clear from their body language that they were furious with each other. Greg kept throwing his hands in the air, while Liza had her hands on her hips, and a huge scowl on her face.

"What should we do?" Cassie asked, grabbing Breezy's sleeve.

"Nothing," Annie decided. "It's between them."

"But we have to do something!" Cassie cried.

Breezy forgot that her ears stuck out and nervously pushed her hair behind them. "But what?"

As the girls skated slowly around the rink, their eyes were glued to Liza and Greg.

And then the worst thing happened.

Liza yelled something at Greg that they couldn't make out, which made Greg fold his arms defiantly.

Then, as the girls watched in horror, he turned around and walked out on his bride-to-be.

8

"What a great job," Annie said sarcastically as she, Cassie, and Breezy walked down the street toward the house Greg and two of his best friends had rented for their senior year of college.

The moms had hired them to walk Greg's dog while Greg and Liza were at a wedding planning meeting with them. "I mean, just think of the glamour of it all. Think of the excitement — "

"Think of the money," Breezy reminded her. "Think of that new hockey gear you want so badly. And the new basketball shoes."

"Besides, we have to prove that ABC Weddings is a professional business," Cassie said, blowing her bangs off her forehead. It was a very hot day, and even though they all had on shorts and T-shirts, they were already sweating. "We want references for other jobs."

"There aren't any other jobs," Annie complained.

"You need to — "

"I know, I know," Annie said. "Think positively."

"Hey, Mrs. Anders called a few days ago," Breezy reminded her. "That could be a job."

Mrs. Anders was the mother of one of Greg's best friends, Pete. In fact, Pete was one of Greg's roommates. Mrs. Anders had called the moms to tell them that her daughter, Crystal, who used to be Breezy's baby-sitter, was getting married, and she wanted to hire the moms to do the wedding. Then she'd called ABC Weddings and asked if the girls could help with the wedding, too. The problem was, she still hadn't given them any dates or any information about the wedding at all.

Which made Breezy wonder if maybe Crystal had called off her wedding.

"Did Crystal ever baby-sit for you?" Breezy asked her friends.

"Don't you remember, my mom used that girl Pam Briar who lived across the street from us," Annie said. "She used to totally ignore me and talk to her boyfriend on the phone. But my parents liked her because they didn't have to drive her home."

"The only sitter I ever had was my cousin," Cassie said as they got closer to the dilapidated brick house Greg and his friends had rented. "All she ever did was watch the Home Shopping Network."

"Crystal used to make paper dolls with me and then we'd design all these clothes for them," Breezy reminisced. "She always told me she was going to be a model one day. And now she really is one!"

"That is so cool," Cassie said. "Can you even imagine, living in New York and being a model? I'll bet the guy she's marrying is as gorgeous as Greg."

"I'll bet they don't fight as much as Liza and Greg," Annie said as they turned up the redbrick walkway to the house.

"I told you, Liza said she and Greg patched things up," Breezy reported.

"You said 'sort of,'" Annie corrected. "They 'sort of' patched things up."

"They're in love, they'll be fine," Cassie said as she reached out to knock on the edge of the screen door. The door inside was open. "This is going to be fun. I love dogs."

Annie liked dogs, too, but she didn't like how obnoxious her brother had been lately. When she'd asked him why one of his roommates couldn't do the walking, Greg had given her one of his typical big-brother superior looks and said a job was a job, wasn't it, and she and her little friends had been hired, hadn't they? So why didn't Annie just do it and be quiet? Annie got angry all over again just remembering how snotty

Greg had been to her. Ever since the day at the roller rink, he had been in a terrible mood.

"No one's answering the door," Cassie said, knocking again.

"I thought you were supposed to be mature before you got married," Annie said. "But my brother is — "

"Oh, wait, you guys!" Breezy interrupted. "I can't believe I almost forgot these."

Breezy rooted around in her small backpack and pulled three T-shirts out of the bag.

"Ta-da!" she sang out, simultaneously tossing one to Annie and another one to Cassie.

"This is so awesome," Cassie said, holding it up in front of her.

Despite the hot weather, Annie quickly pulled hers on over the T-shirt she was already wearing. So did Cassie and Breezy.

Annie looked down at herself, then admired her friends. She swung Cassie around so she could see her from the back.

"Breezer, I gotta admit, these are cool in a major way," Annie said.

The T-shirts were bright pink, and on the back, in silk-screened large white letters, they read ABC WEDDINGS. And then, on the front each shirt had a name embroidered in pale pink thread.

"Oh, Breezy, thanks, these are amazing!" Cassie said, hugging her hard.

"Don't thank me," Breezy said, "thank my aunt Faith. She had them made for us."

"Thank you, Aunt Faith!" Annie shouted.

"We look really official now," Cassie said proudly.

"We are official," Annie said.

"Right. So, let's get the pooches," Breezy commanded.

"Try ringing the doorbell instead of knocking," Annie suggested.

Cassie rang the bell. Instantly, from inside the house, came a howling, barking, baying racket.

"The dogs?" Cassie asked a little nervously.

"You got it," Annie said.

"Do they bite?" Cassie asked anxiously.

"Not as bad as Brett the Biter," Annie said with a shrug.

Greg's roommate came to the door. He was on crutches and his right leg was in a cast, which explained why he couldn't take the dogs out for a walk himself.

"Hi, Annie," he said, letting them into the house.

"This is one of Greg's roommates, Pete Anders," Annie told her friends.

"So, you guys are the bridal buddies, huh?" Pete asked.

"ABC Weddings," Breezy said. "At your service." She turned around so he could see the back of her shirt.

"Cool T-shirts," he told them.

"Thanks. So, we heard your sister, Crystal, is getting married," Breezy said, hoping to get some more information, and another job for ABC Weddings.

"I heard the same rumor," Pete said.

"You mean you don't know if she's getting married or not?" Annie asked him.

Pete shrugged. "When it comes to Crystal, I am the last one to know anything. I think she told my mom she had to go to Paris on some big fashion shoot. . . . "

"Paris?" Cassie breathed. "She's modeling in Paris, France?"

Pete shrugged again. "I guess. So, I'm sure you guys want to see the dogs, huh?" He whistled through his teeth, and three dogs came charging into the front hallway. One was a Saint Bernard, gigantic, slobbering, and well over a hundred pounds. One was a gorgeous golden retriever, about fifty pounds. The last dog was a tiny Chihuahua about the size of a small dinner plate.

"Oh, the little one is so cute!" Cassie cried as the tiny dog jumped against her leg.

"Just wait," Annie said. And, as if she had been telling the future, the three dogs started yapping, barking, and howling all over again.

"Quiet!" Pete thundered at the dogs. The two larger dogs were silenced, but the Chihuahua only barked more loudly, running in circles around the girls.

"Sit!" Pete commanded the little dog sternly. The dog finally obeyed. He looked up at the girls. "So, here they are. Bring 'em back in an hour." He turned and hobbled away on his crutches.

"That's it?" Breezy called after him.

"What else is there?" Pete said. Then he turned back to them. "Oh, yeah. The town just passed a pooper-scooper law. You have to clean up after 'em."

He reached for something on the table in the hall and threw it toward the girls. It was a small box of plastic bags.

"Gee, thanks," Annie said, making the catch.

Pete waved and hobbled into the family room.

Breezy spotted the dogs' leashes hanging on hooks near the door.

"Well, let's get to work," she said, taking one of the leashes and attaching it to the Saint Bernard's collar. Cassie and Annie followed suit — Annie taking the golden retriever and Cassie the Chihuahua.

"Their names are on their leash-hooks," Annie pointed out. "The big, slobbery one is Tiny, the retriever's name is Minnie, and the obnoxious yappy little one's name is Four-Oh-Nine."

"Oh, you hurt his feelings," Cassie said, bending down to give the littlest dog a kiss. "Four-Oh-Nine? Is your name Four-Oh-Nine?" The tiny

Chihuahua responded with fifteen or twenty loud yaps and slurpy kisses.

"What kind of name is that?" Breezy asked.

"It's what he weighs!" Pete shouted from the other room. "Four pounds, nine ounces!"

"Right," Annie shouted back. "Great dog!"

Four-Oh-Nine drooled on Cassie's new T-shirt.

"I thought you said the big one was the drooler," Cassie said, quickly putting the little dog down.

"All dogs drool when it's this hot," Annie said.

"Okay, ABC Weddings," Breezy said, "let's get this show on the road."

The dogs seemed to understand what Breezy had just said. They made a mad dash for the door, pulling the three girls after them.

9

"Thank goodness they're finally tired," Cassie said with exhaustion. She plopped down next to Four-Oh-Nine on the grass of the park about ten blocks from Greg's house. Although the sun had been out for a while, it had rained earlier in the day, and some of the areas in the park were still wet. But the dogs had picked out a dry spot to do a little sunbathing.

Not that the girls cared. They were too tired to care. The dogs had run them ragged for the past forty-five minutes.

Annie and Breezy sat down next to Cassie. Breezy lay on her back. Some sweat dripped into her eye. "I am beyond pooped."

"Me too, but I still love this little guy," Cassie said, petting Four-Oh-Nine, who gave her some more doggy kisses. "Which dog belongs to Greg?"

"Tiny," Annie replied, holding fast to the huge dog's leash. "And frankly, ever since the wed-

66

ding plans started, I kind of prefer Tiny to my brother."

Breezy pulled up a piece of grass and twirled it between her fingers. "Liza's been really unhappy, too."

"What did Greg do now?" Annie asked. She rested her head on the huge body of the Saint Bernard as if it were a pillow.

Cassie tickled Four-Oh-Nine with a blade of grass. "I thought you said they made up."

"They did," Breezy said. "But now . . . well, the truth is, they're fighting again."

"That's terrible," Cassie said. She rested her head on her hands, Four-Oh-Nine's leash lying loosely in her palm.

"I know," Breezy agreed. "I didn't want to tell you guys, but . . . I think it's worse than ever. Liza's guest list has grown to something like a hundred and fifty people. And she went with the moms to Chicago to pick out her wedding gown — "

"Why didn't she go to my parents' shop?" Cassie asked, feeling hurt.

"Liza wanted this really expensive designer gown that some shop in Chicago carries," Breezy explained. "I hope that doesn't hurt your feelings, Cass."

"No," Cassie fibbed. "Maybe she didn't know that my parents' shop has some really expensive gowns."

"She *did* hurt your feelings," Breezy realized. "I'm sorry, Cassie."

"It's okay," Cassie said, trying hard to mean it. "But it would have been fun to help her pick out her gown."

Annie absentmindedly scratched Tiny behind the ears. "So, go on with your story," she urged Breezy.

"Well, Greg hasn't seen the gown, of course," Breezy continued, "but he heard how much it cost and then he went ballistic."

"But he's not paying for it, your parents are," Annie pointed out.

"I know," Breezy agreed. "It's just the idea of it. Greg told Liza it was obscene to spend that kind of money on a dress she would only wear once."

"He could be a little more romantic about it," Cassie observed.

Breezy nodded in agreement. "He said he thought they should take the money our parents are spending on the wedding and use it for graduate school or a down payment on a house, or something practical."

"He could be a *lot* more romantic about it," Cassie corrected herself.

Tiny slurped Annie's hand. "It sounds kind of smart to me," Annie said.

"Smart?" Cassie repeated.

"Well, why spend thousands and thousands of

68

dollars on something that lasts a few hours when you could use the money for something really important?"

"A wedding *is* really important!" Cassie insisted. "How can you say that?"

"You guys, don't argue," Breezy said wearily.

"Well, at least Greg is with Liza and the moms right now," Cassie said. "At least he's trying."

"True," Breezy agreed. "But being there and wanting to be there are two different things."

"Agreed," Annie said, grimacing as she wiped her slobber-covered hand on her shorts. "For instance, I'm here with the three canine slobber kings of Summerville, but I'd rather be home watching the Cubs play on television."

"A few more jobs like this and we can go to Chicago and watch the Cubs play for real," Breezy pointed out.

"So what are we going to do about Greg?" Cassie asked, looking pointedly at Annie.

"Hey, he's just my brother," Annie said. "I can't make him get excited about something he doesn't care about."

"Doesn't care about!" Cassie cried. "Annie, it's his one and only wedding! There has to be something we can do to — "

At that moment, Cassie felt the leash slide off the palm of her hand as Four-Oh-Nine tore off toward the far end of the park, his leash trailing behind him.

"I thought you were holding his leash!" Annie cried, scrambling to her feet.

"I was," Cassie said as she got up, too. "I didn't know he was going to run all of a sudden!"

"We've got to catch him!" Breezy exclaimed.

The three girls took off, the other two dogs' leashes in hand, chasing after Four-Oh-Nine. But Annie and Breezy were held back by Tiny and Minnie, who were all run out and just wanted to dawdle and sniff the grass.

Cassie ran ahead on her own, her heart pounding. If Four-Oh-Nine was going to be caught, she'd be the one who'd have to catch him. And if he wasn't caught, it would be all her fault, and ABC Weddings would be out of business forever.

"Four-Oh-Nine, oh Four-Oh-Nine!" Cassie yelled. She pumped her legs as fast as she could after the Chihuahua. Just when she seemed to be gaining on the dog, he cut across the children's playground and headed off toward a skateboard park and, beyond that, the soccer field.

"Come back!" Cassie yelled frantically at the dog, who was getting farther and farther ahead of her. Desperately, she forced herself to run even faster, her arms pumping, sweat running down her face.

That's when she felt her legs go flying out from under her.

A split second later, she was on her stomach, facedown in a huge mud puddle.

She lay there, stupefied, covered in mud, breathing hard. Four-Oh-Nine was nowhere to be seen. All she could think was that because of her, their wedding business was ruined. No one would ever hire them again after they found out that, because of her, Greg's roommate's dog had run away. And no one would even speak to her again if they found out that, because of her, a sweet little doggie named Four-Oh-Nine was lost somewhere in the —

"Cassie!" Breezy yelled when she and Annie finally caught up to her. "Are you okay?"

Cassie struggled to get to her feet. She tried to wipe the mud out of her eyes, but her hands were so muddy that she only made it worse. "I lost Four-Oh-Nine," she cried miserably.

"You look like you just made a headfirst slide trying to steal second base," Annie said, trying not to laugh at her mud-covered friend.

"It isn't funny," Cassie said, practically in tears. "What are we going to do about — "

But Annie's eyes weren't on Cassie. And neither were Breezy's. They were looking past her, behind her.

"What?" Cassie asked. She turned around to see what they were looking at.

And what she saw made her want to sink back down into that mud puddle and never come up for air.

Because standing there on his skateboard, with

Four-Oh-Nine in his arms, looking impossibly cute, was David Silver.

He stepped off his skateboard and held the dog out to mud-covered Cassie. "Does this dog belong to you?"

"David?" Cassie squeaked. Her hand went up to her hair. All she felt was mud.

"The dog was running by me and I heard you yelling, so I . . . " David didn't finish his sentence. He just handed Cassie the little dog.

"Thanks," Cassie said. "I . . . uh . . . fell."

Annie snorted back a laugh. Breezy nudged her in the ribs.

"So . . . " Cassie said, feeling like an idiot. A gooey clump of mud slithered into her right eye.

"Well, bye," David said. He got back onto his skateboard and fled.

"Please tell me that didn't just happen," Cassie begged her friends.

But they couldn't tell her it hadn't happened, because of course it had. And even though Breezy and Annie knew Cassie was beyond embarrassed, and they really tried not to laugh, finally they couldn't help themselves.

Two laughing girls, three dogs, and one mud-covered Cassie trudged back to Greg's house, leaving a trail of muddy footprints behind them.

10

"**A**n outdoor wedding?" Annie's mom asked, giving her son, Greg, a dirty look.

"Lots of people have outdoor weddings, Mom," Annie said, answering for her brother, whose face was hidden behind the sports page of the *Indianapolis Star*, the local newspaper.

It was a week later, and Annie was tired of listening to her mom arguing with Greg and Greg arguing with Liza. It was always about the same thing.

The wedding.

It was getting incredibly annoying.

Annie shoved some more oatmeal into her mouth. Yuck. Her parents had read somewhere that oatmeal was really healthy, and now they expected her to eat it for breakfast every other day. Cassie ate oatmeal for breakfast because she actually *liked* it. But Annie's favorite breakfast was cold pizza with everything on it. Oatmeal just could not compete.

Mrs. McGee reached across the breakfast table and pulled the newspaper down so she could see her son's face.

"What are you going to do if it rains, Greg? Answer me that."

"Bring an umbrella," Greg said, lifting the newspaper again.

Mrs. McGee pointed at him in frustration. "You are being impossible, Greg."

Greg put down the newspaper. "Look, Mom, for once Liza and I agree about something. We don't want to get married at Pine Woods Country Club. It's just not our style. We want to have the wedding outside. So Annie and her little friends are going to go scout us the perfect location today. Right, Annie?"

"Right," Annie agreed, letting some oatmeal drip off her spoon into her bowl. "But only if you stop calling Cassie and Breezy my 'little friends.' We're a professional business. We get paid."

While Paula McGee continued to argue with her son over the location of the wedding, Annie took the opportunity to sneak her oatmeal bowl into the sink, where she dumped the majority of the glop down the garbage disposal. She knew Breezy would have some kind of junk food at her house, and that was exactly where she was heading.

"Okay, so I'm outta here," Annie called in to her mom.

Mrs. McGee came out into the hall. Her face was pinched with anxiety. Annie sighed. Why was it that her mom always seemed to be so stressed out? No one else in the family was like that.

"Listen," her mom said, "don't worry if you girls don't find the perfect outdoor spot for the wedding, because — "

"Mom, we've got a job to do," Annie cut in. "We're biking over to the Botanical Gardens. There must be lots of great spots for a wedding there."

Greg walked by and pulled the bill of Annie's baseball cap down lower on her forehead. "Find us something great, kiddo. Thanks for breakfast," he said as he walked toward the front door.

"Greg, where are you going?" his mother called to him.

"Over to Liza's," Greg said. He stopped and turned to her. "And Mom, please try to remember that I'm twenty-one years old. Okay?"

"I know," Mrs. McGee said. "I know you're all grown up and I know it's your wedding. But you can't blame Stephanie and me for wanting it to be perfect. It's our business. And you're our kids."

"Just remember that perfect for the two of you might not be perfect for me and Liza," Greg said gently. "Okay?"

Mrs. McGee nodded in agreement, but she didn't look too happy about it.

"Man, I just wish she'd lay off," Greg said as he

and Annie headed outside into the bright sunlight. He put on his sunglasses.

"She's nervous," Annie said.

"Yeah, what else is new," Greg agreed.

"You'll be nervous when your kid is getting married, too, I'll bet," Annie told him.

Greg shook his head from side to side. "Don't even mention kids to me! I can barely handle the wedding thing, much less kids."

Annie scratched a mosquito bite on her shin. "Well, you don't have to have kids for a long time. If you want kids, I mean."

"Who knows," Greg muttered, staring off into the distance. He focused on Annie again. "Take a tip from me, kiddo. When you decide to get married, elope." He got into his car and looked at her out the open window.

Annie got on her bike. "I'm never getting married," she called to him.

"You know, that's a great idea," Greg said.

Annie kicked up her kickstand. "You're kidding, right?" She grinned at him nervously. "I mean, you love Liza. And Liza loves you."

"What's love got to do with it?" Greg asked. Then he started his car and drove off.

Annie just stood there a minute, her legs on either side of her bike, watching her brother's car disappear down the street. Did Greg really think that not getting married was a good idea?

* * *

"According to this map, if we go down that path, we'll reach an open area with a small water-fall," Cassie said, pointing to a gravel path to their right. She looked down again at the map they'd been given when they entered the gardens.

"Did Jennifer star it?" Breezy asked, leaning over to look at the map. Jennifer was the college student whose summer job was to sit at the welcome desk at the front entrance of the gardens. She was really nice and very helpful. She told them she was studying to be a botanist — a scientist who works with plants. And she starred the map at the two spots in the gardens that she thought would be best for an outdoor wedding.

"Uh-huh," Cassie said. "See."

"Okay, so let's go," Breezy said. "Maybe we should walk our bikes. It's all uphill and rocky."

The three of them walked their bikes uphill on the gravelly road.

"How's Liza supposed to get up this hill in her wedding dress?" Cassie asked. "Besides, what if she sweats her makeup off?"

"Let's just reserve judgment until we find the spot," Breezy said, wiping some sweat off her forehead.

Finally, they reached a large clearing. The spot was so beautiful, it took their breath away.

"Wow," Breezy breathed, taking it all in.

"Double wow," Annie echoed.

Huge trees bowed over the road on both sides, creating a canopy of green. Just beyond the trees was a lawn area surrounded by beautifully kept gardens, with bright flowers of every hue swaying in the slight breeze. And beyond that was the brook that ran through the nature preserve. Here it dropped into a small waterfall about ten feet high. The cool, clear water danced over the stones. The only sounds were the rush of the waterfall and the chirping of the many birds that flew overhead.

"This is paradise," Cassie declared, looking around. "This is how I imagine heaven or something, except without the walk."

"The ceremony could take place right over there on the lawn," Breezy said, pointing. She was picturing everything in her mind.

"And then the moms could set up big open tents over there, where the food could be served," Cassie said, getting excited just thinking about it. "And a string quartet could play right over there." She pointed to a spot in front of the flower garden. "It's just so perfect!"

"I agree, but I think the moms are thinking about having just the ceremony here," Breezy explained.

"So where does everyone go after the service, then?" Cassie asked.

"The country club," Breezy admitted.

Annie's jaw fell open. "Wait a minute. Greg

didn't say anything about that. He said he and Liza didn't want to have anything at the country club. He said it isn't their style."

Breezy shrugged. "Maybe I'm wrong. Ask the moms."

"Don't you think this spot is perfect for the ceremony?" Cassie asked Annie.

"It's okay," Annie said.

Cassie was incredulous. "Okay? It's only the most beautiful spot I ever saw in my whole life!"

Annie shrugged. She had been so eager to get over to Breezy's house so that she could tell her friends what Greg had said that morning, but the weird thing was that once she had gotten there, she hadn't said anything at all. It was as if she felt she was being disloyal to Greg or something. But that was crazy. First of all, she couldn't stand him, and second of all, it was Breezy's sister he was marrying.

That is, if Greg didn't call the whole thing off.

"Annie, what's up?" Breezy asked. "You've been really quiet all afternoon."

"And you're never really quiet," Cassie added.

Annie put the kickstand down on her bike and sat on the grass. "I have to tell you guys something."

"Is it something bad?" Cassie asked as she and Breezy sat down next to her.

Annie struggled with herself. "It's really private. And I feel funny telling you, but — "

"Oh, no!" Cassie cried. "You're in love with David Silver and you don't want to hurt my feelings. That's it, isn't it?"

"No, that isn't it," Annie said with disgust. "This secret isn't even about me."

"Oh," was all Cassie could manage. She was horribly embarrassed. "Sorry."

Breezy patted Cassie's knee.

"It's about Greg and Liza. And their wedding," Annie said. She let her fingers brush against the tickly grass underneath her.

"Did they have another fight?" Cassie asked.

"I don't know," Annie replied. "What I have to tell you guys is what Greg said to me this morning." Then she told them, word for word, leaving nothing out.

"I don't think Greg really meant he didn't want to get married," Breezy said when Annie had finished.

Annie shrugged. "He sounded like he meant it."

"But he loves Liza!" Cassie protested. "He couldn't have meant that he didn't want to get married. Could he?"

"I don't know," Annie said, sighing. "But I do know that ever since they started planning this wedding, Greg and Liza fight all the time. And if you argue all the time, what's the point of getting married?"

"It's just stress," Breezy said, trying to convince herself.

80

"Right," Cassie agreed uncertainly. She stood up. "I say we go back to your house, Breezy, and tell Liza and Greg we've found them the perfect spot for the ceremony and reception. Or just the ceremony. Or . . . well, however they want to do it. That should make them happy."

Annie and Breezy got up, and the three of them turned their bikes around and began to walk them down the gravel road.

They didn't say much, but they were all worried about the same thing.

What if Greg was serious?

What if the wedding really was off?

11

"Hey, Mom, are Liza and Greg here?" Breezy asked her mom, who was sitting on the front porch rocker, going over some bills. The three girls looked expectantly at Mrs. Zeeman.

"In the family room," Mrs. Zeeman said, noting something on one of the bills. "Talking."

"Talking or arguing?" Annie asked, sitting down in one of the other rocking chairs.

Mrs. Zeeman lifted her head from the pile of bills. "I don't know, to tell you the truth. I've tried to steer clear of them all morning. When I went into the kitchen to get some lemonade, I heard them, but I'm really trying not to interfere."

"I wish you'd tell my mom that," Annie said, popping some bubble gum into her mouth.

"Come on," Breezy told her friends. "Let's go see what's up."

"I don't want you girls to interfere, either," Mrs. Zeeman cautioned them.

"Never happen," Annie assured her.

Breezy led her friends through her house and into the family room. They heard Greg and Liza before they saw them.

"What do you mean it's my fault?" Liza cried. "Is it a crime to want to make my mother happy?"

"You're marrying me, not your mother," Greg stormed. "Grow up, Liza!"

"Don't talk to me like that," Liza fumed.

The girls stood in the archway of the family room, slack-jawed. Greg and Liza were standing in the middle of the room, in the midst of a fight so huge they didn't even notice that anyone else was there.

"You're driving me nuts, Liza," Greg said, running his hand through his hair.

"Well, I'm sorry if what I want upsets you, but — "

"It's like you're turning into someone I don't even know!" Greg yelled. "What happened to the girl who hangs out in sweats and goes camping with me?"

"Nothing! And that has nothing to do with the kind of wedding I want, Greg! Why are you being so pigheaded?"

"Me?" Greg asked incredulously. "What about you? And what about — "

Breezy cleared her throat, and Greg and Liza turned toward the girls.

"Great timing," Greg mumbled.

Liza sank down on the couch and buried her head in her hands.

Breezy looked helplessly at her friends, then turned back to Greg and Liza. "So . . . we have really good news!"

"I could use some," Liza said wearily.

Greg sat down next to her, but not very close.

"We found the most perfect place for your wedding," Cassie told them brightly. "It's so beautiful and so romantic."

"And it's outdoors, just like you wanted," Breezy added. She looked over at Annie, urging her with her eyes to chime in, but Annie remained silent.

"So, isn't that great news?" Cassie asked meekly.

"Great," Greg said. His voice was completely flat.

"That *is* what you wanted," Annie said, looking at her brother. "Isn't it?"

"Sure," he said tonelessly.

Liza looked at her fiancé with tears in her eyes. "Why are you acting like this, Greg?"

"Like what?"

"Like you don't care," Liza said, swallowing back her tears. "Like . . . like you don't even want to get married."

Greg sighed. "Liza, we need to talk." He looked over at the girls. "Could the three of you please get lost?"

"We're going," Annie assured him.

As the girls tiptoed out of the room, they were in a state of shock. Quickly they all ran up to their clubhouse.

"This is terrible," Cassie cried, hugging a giant pillow to her. "He's going to call off the wedding!"

"Do you really think so?" Breezy said anxiously.

Annie put her head in her hands. "It's all my stupid brother's fault."

"There must be something we can do," Cassie moaned. Then she got an idea. "Breezy, you have a photo of Liza and Greg in your photo album, right?"

"The photo album is right over there," Breezy said, standing up and getting her album from the shelves in the corner of the room. "How come?"

"Get their photo, and put it in the hope chest."

Breezy took the photo album and looked through it, finding a photo of her sister and Greg together at some college party.

"Why am I doing this, Cassie?" Breezy asked as she opened the hope chest and dropped the photo inside.

Cassie put her hand on her heart. "Because our most private, special hopes and dreams are in the hope chest. And if we join hands and think the most positive thoughts for Greg and Liza, maybe Greg won't call off the wedding."

"That is unbelievably lame," Annie said flatly. "We need a better plan than that."

"Let's just do it," Breezy urged her friend. "It can't hurt."

"Do you have a better idea?" Cassie asked Annie.

"Not really," Annie admitted. She reached over to close the top of the hope chest, and then held her hands out to her friends. Then they all closed their eyes.

"We know that Greg and Liza truly love each other," Cassie said. "So please let them work out their problems and have the most beautiful wedding in the world." She opened her eyes. Her friends were gazing at her skeptically.

"Now we have to picture their perfect wedding," she told them.

"This is beyond dumb," Annie said.

"It is not. I saw it on TV," Cassie insisted. "It's called positive mental imaging. If we can imagine it, we can help make it true."

They all shut their eyes again and concentrated on the perfect wedding for Liza and Greg.

Annie didn't know how her friends felt, but as for her, she had a terrible, scary feeling deep inside, and for once she felt as anxious as her mother.

Because unless they came up with something better than a picture in a hope chest and some wishful thinking, Annie was really afraid that Liza and Greg's wedding was never going to be.

12

"You guys won't believe this," Annie said as she barreled out of the revolving door and into Summerville Hospital, where she was meeting Cassie and Breezy. Her friends were already waiting for her in the hospital visitors' area, located right inside the front doors.

"You're late," Breezy said, pointing to her watch.

"What, like five minutes," Annie replied.

"Fifteen minutes," Breezy said. She looked at her watch again. "Sixteen."

Annie shook her head. "You know, Breezer, you really need to get over this perfectionist thing. I mean, just because you have to be perfect doesn't mean that I do, too. Hey, are Greg and Liza here yet?" she added.

"Not yet," Cassie replied. "I hope that isn't a bad sign."

"The wedding is still on," Breezy pointed out.

That was a big thing in and of itself. They had

all felt certain that Greg was going to tell Liza he was calling off the wedding. When it hadn't happened, Cassie insisted that the "positive imaging" they had done in the clubhouse a few weeks earlier, when they had put the photo of Liza and Greg in their hope chest, had worked.

"It's less than a month away now," Cassie said, smoothing her bangs down on her forehead. "If they can only last until the wedding . . . "

"They still fight all the time," Annie said gloomily. "Every day I think Greg is going to tell us that the whole thing is off. I truly do not see why people even get married. I'm sick of the whole thing."

Breezy was feeling kind of sick of the whole thing, too. Liza was so tense that everyone in the Zeeman household felt as if they were walking on eggshells around her. One minute Liza would be all happy and glowing, and the next minute she'd be in tears. Frankly, it was exhausting.

Still, the girls were hopeful. They felt certain that if Liza and Greg could just manage to make it until the wedding, the big stresses would be over, and they'd stop bickering and live happily ever after.

They all thought it was a good sign, for example, that Liza and Greg were going to do their usual volunteer work at the hospital that day. Because Greg and Liza had been so busy and stressed out, the moms had hired ABC Weddings to take the bridal couple's place at the hospital and entertain the little kids. But just the day before, Greg and Liza had told the girls that they didn't want to disappoint the kids who had been in the hospital a long time and who loved their visits. So they were going to come along, too.

On a three-way phone call the night before, the girls all agreed this was a great sign. Surely a couple who didn't want to disappoint sick little kids was a couple meant to be together forever. And besides, the moms were going to pay ABC Weddings anyway.

For Cassie, there was an added bonus. She had found out from Breezy's mom that David Silver's little sister, five-year-old Melody, was in the hospital because of complications from having her tonsils removed. She was embarrassed to admit it, but even being near a relative of David's made Cassie feel excited.

"So, what was it you were yelling about when you came in?" Breezy asked Annie, leaning against the wall as an orderly wheeled a woman in a wheelchair past them.

"Check this out." Annie reached into her back pocket and pulled out a much-folded sheet of paper. She thrust it in front of Cassie and Breezy.

"Where'd you get this?" Cassie asked, looking down at it.

"The kitchen garbage," Annie admitted sheepishly. "It was right on top. It's not like I stole it."

Breezy and Cassie leaned over to look at the paper more closely. It was a photocopy of a memo from Mrs. McGee to Mrs. Zeeman.

PERFECT WEDDINGS
Zeeman/McGee Wedding
Preliminary Plan Memo

Stephanie —

This is to confirm the preliminary plan for the wedding. The wedding will be in the Botanical Gardens. G will arrive by limo, B by white horse-drawn carriage. There will be a maid of honor, a best man, six B/maids, six G/men, two junior B/maids, two flower girls, and one ring bearer. Guest list is 266, divided equally between bride and groom. B and G will enter through split ranks of Summerville High marching band. Ceremony will be under a tent erected in grove located by ABC Weddings. Following ceremony, horse-drawn carriages will take wedding party back to country club. Guests will follow in their own cars. Five-course sit-down dinner with two alternating bands: Rock Around the Clock, who do rock oldies and some standards, and Fired Up, who do current rock. Wedding cake shipped in from New York. Honeymoon limo taking them to airport for flight to Los Angeles and Hawaii to pick up B/G at two in the morning, at the reception.

Any changes, let's discuss.

— Paula

"Wow," was all Breezy could manage.

"You think Greg has agreed to all of this?" Annie asked them.

"The moms wouldn't plan it if he hadn't agreed," Breezy said. But in her heart, she didn't feel totally certain.

"What an incredible wedding!" Cassie exclaimed, her eyes shining. She looked over at her friends. "You two are so lucky to be junior bridesmaids."

"You wouldn't say that if you saw our dresses," Annie said, shuddering.

Just the day before, she and Breezy had gone for their final fitting. The satin dresses were floorlength and pale pink, with ruffles at the neckline and puffy short sleeves.

"I don't mind the dress that much," Breezy said. "But we have to wear our hair up off our faces, with matching pink satin ribbons. My ears will stick out like pie plates."

Annie looked down at the memo again. "The Summerville High marching band? Why don't the moms just rent out the RCA Dome and the whole Colts football team?"

"Probably they couldn't afford it," Cassie replied.

Annie gave her a jaded look. "I think you're missing my point. I just don't believe Greg has agreed to all of this. And I don't blame him! This is totally over the top! No wonder he — "

Annie cut off her own sentence as Greg and Liza came into the hospital. For once, they were hand in hand and not arguing.

"Sorry we're late," Liza said. "We got stuck at the photographers'."

Cassie smiled at them. "We understand. You two have a lot to think about."

"We brought our clowning stuff with us," Greg said, holding up a bag. "But let's go see the kids before we change, because we're so late."

When they reached the pediatrics lounge on the fourth floor, a group of about twenty kids, some of them on crutches or in wheelchairs, were waiting for them. The kids gave a loud cheer of welcome. Even the two nurses joined in.

"Yay!" a little girl in a wheelchair cried, clapping her hands together. She looked over at her friend, a handsome boy on crutches who stood next to her. "I told you they'd come, Miguel!"

Greg knelt down and gave the little girl a kiss on her cheek. "Hi there, Sharon. How could I stay away from my favorite girl?"

"You gonna do clowning and stuff?" Miguel asked eagerly. "Hey, remember you said you'd teach me to juggle!"

"You got it," Greg assured him. "Liza and I are going to go change into our magic clown costumes. We'll be right back." Greg grabbed Liza's hand and they went around the corner to change.

"You guys, did you see how well Liza and Greg are getting along?" Cassie asked her friends excitedly.

"They aren't fighting," Breezy agreed.

"Maybe it's the calm before the storm," Annie put in.

Cassie folded her arms. "You know, you really could look on the bright side sometimes. It wouldn't hurt you."

"I guess," Annie agreed reluctantly, taking her Nerf ball out of her back pocket. She threw it to Sharon. The little girl caught it and happily threw it back.

Cassie smiled dreamily. She was sure everything would be fine now. Greg really was wonderful. Just like David Silver. One day she and David would be madly in love, and they would work together to make little kids happy, and —

Cassie's reverie was interrupted by what she saw across the room, in the far corner of the lounge.

No. It couldn't be.

But it was.

Cassie leaned over and grabbed Breezy's hand. "David Silver is sitting on the other side of the room!" she hissed in Breezy's ear.

Breezy turned around to look.

"Don't be so obvious!" Cassie begged in a frantic whisper.

"I guess he's visiting his sister," Breezy said.

She waved to David, who was sitting on a couch with Melody.

David waved back. Cassie pretended to be too busy fixing the tiny loops in her pierced ears to notice.

"Breezy, what am I going to do?" Cassie asked desperately, sliding her eyes over to David again.

"Just be yourself," Breezy advised her.

"I hate it when people say that!" Cassie exclaimed. "If I knew how to 'be myself,' why would I be asking you what I should do?"

"We want the show!" one of the little kids yelped.

"We want the show!" Miguel chimed in. The kids got noisier and noisier. Even Sharon, who was still playing catch with Annie, joined in.

One of the nurses came over to the girls. "Maybe you girls could start to entertain the kids while Greg and Liza are changing," she suggested. "Some of them can't stay up too long."

"You got it," Annie said.

Before the girls knew that Liza and Greg would be coming to the hospital, they had planned to do a sing-along with the kids to get things started.

"Yo! You guys, over here!" Annie called.

The kids stopped talking and stared at Annie. "Hi," she greeted them. "My name is Annie, and these are my buds, Breezy and Cassie."

"Hi," Sharon said, smiling shyly. Some of the other kids said hi, too.

"We'd like to teach you a song," Cassie went on. "How many of you know 'Row, Row, Row Your Boat'?"

"That's a stupid song," a bigger boy in the back yelled. He was wearing Batman pajamas and a baseball cap over his bald head.

Bald from chemotherapy drugs that you get if you have cancer, Cassie figured. She had a cousin who had had cancer, which was how she knew about it. Her cousin had gotten all better, and all her hair had grown back, too.

"Yeah, stupid," another kid agreed. A bunch of other kids joined in. Singing was definitely not what they wanted to do.

Cassie snuck another look over at David. He was sitting with his arm around Melody, watching her. She quickly looked away.

"Well, we could do something else, then," Cassie said. "Like . . . uh . . . " Her mind was a total blank. She looked at Breezy and Annie for help.

"We want clowns!" Sharon yelled out.

"Are you guys clowns?" another kid asked.

"Uh . . . not really," Breezy admitted.

"We want Greg and Liza!" Miguel said.

"Right," Breezy agreed. "So . . . I'll go see if Liza and Greg are ready." She hurried out of the room while Cassie and Annie tried, and failed, to get the kids to sing "This Old Man."

"I guess a sing-along wasn't the greatest idea in the world," Breezy mumbled to herself as she rounded the corner, where she almost smacked into Greg and Liza, who were so busy arguing they didn't even notice that Breezy was there. Their bag of clowning stuff lay at their feet — they hadn't even changed into their clown outfits yet.

Breezy listened as they argued in low, cold tones.

"Why did you have to pick the most deluxe photography package they offered us, can you answer me that?"

"Those are memories we'll keep forever," Liza replied.

"Liza, this whole thing is making me crazy. It's gotten totally out of hand. A cake from New York? A marching band? This isn't a wedding, it's a circus!"

Liza looked as if she was ready to cry. "Why do you have to keep doing this, Greg? It's like you don't care about my dreams at all."

"Well, since when have you shown that you care about mine?" Greg shot back.

"What dreams? All you do is complain. What else is bugging you? You might as well get it all out!"

"Okay, I will," Greg said. Two passing nurses had to walk around him, but he didn't even notice.

"Let's talk honeymoon. My parents are giving us a check for five thousand dollars for the honeymoon. Do you know what we could do with that money, instead of going first-class to Hawaii?"

"It's supposed to be romantic," Liza said, hurt.

"I'd rather save the money, go up to Maine, rent a Jeep, and bomb around for a couple of weeks."

"Maine?" Liza asked archly.

"Absolutely," Greg said. "I know you love to camp. And fish. We go all the time."

"Not on my *honeymoon*!"

The argument showed no signs of ending. And Breezy was pretty certain that the two of them were not going to put on a show for the kids anytime soon. What could she do? The sing-along concept was not going to work, that was for sure.

Impetuously, Breezy grabbed their bag of clowning stuff. Greg and Liza stopped in midargument and looked at Breezy with surprise.

"Don't worry," Breezy assured them. "We've got everything under control in there. Everything is . . . fine. Really." She hurried back toward the lounge, just praying that she had told the truth. But before she even got close, she could hear the little kids screaming and complaining, totally out of control.

Breezy had absolutely no idea what to do.

13

The lounge was bedlam. Cassie and Annie were still trying to lead a sing-along, but the kids were singing totally different songs from the one Cassie was desperately trying to get them to sing. A toddler in the corner was crying while a nurse tried to comfort him. Other kids were screaming at the top of their lungs for no apparent reason at all. In the back of the room, Melody had her hands over her ears and her head buried in her big brother's chest.

"David is going to think I'm an idiot," Cassie told Annie.

"Forget David," Annie snapped. "These kids are ready to operate on us without anesthetic!"

"We want clowns!" Sharon yelled from her wheelchair. Other kids took up the chant.

"We want clowns! We want clowns!"

"I think this show is over," a stern-faced nurse told Annie and Cassie. "We're taking the kids back to their rooms."

"But, but . . . we really can entertain them," Cassie protested helplessly. "I think."

Two more nurses hurried in to help get the kids back to their rooms, but at the same moment, Breezy bounded through the door carrying Greg and Liza's clowning bag. "You want clowns, you got it!" she shouted back to the children. Quickly, she reached into the bag and gave an astonished Cassie and Annie a couple of masks and a couple of clown props each.

"Ta-da!" Breezy sang out. "ABC Weddings is proud to present . . . the Clown Show!"

"What are we doing?" Annie asked Breezy under her breath.

"We'll make it up as we go along," Breezy muttered back.

"Please don't make me look stupid in front of David," Cassie begged.

"Do some gymnastics," Breezy whispered to Annie.

"What?"

"Just do it!" Breezy smiled at the kids. "Okay, kids!" she called to them. "Please welcome the incredible, unbelievable clown, Acrobatic Annie!"

"Do something!" Cassie hissed at Annie.

Annie stood on her hands. Then she did a back flip. Then she turned three cartwheels in a row.

Thankfully, the kids applauded. Annie did some more tricks while Breezy made up a running narration. "For Acrobatic Annie's next trick, she's going to do a handstand on one hand!"

Annie gave her a look. Sometimes she could do a one-handed handstand, and sometimes she couldn't. Fortunately, she pulled it off.

As the kids applauded, Cassie rummaged quickly through the clown stuff to see if she could find anything to help them.

She found a large package of balloons. Years ago, her dad had taught her to make balloon animals. Just as the kids were getting tired of Annie's gymnastics, Cassie began to create balloon animals, which she handed out to the kids in the room. They loved it, and begged to learn how to make their own.

A half hour later, when Liza and Greg finally came into the lounge, they found that ABC Weddings was doing a terrific job entertaining all the sick kids. Everywhere they looked, kids were holding balloon animals. A couple of girls had made balloon hats and wore them on their heads.

"Thanks," Liza told Breezy gratefully. "I'm sorry we . . . " Liza's voice trailed off. She looked as if she was going to cry.

Breezy reached for her sister's arm and gave her a friendly squeeze. "Don't worry about it," Breezy assured her. "Really."

Liza gave Breezy a grateful smile. It was so weird. For just a moment there, Breezy felt as if she were Liza's big sister, instead of the other way around.

*   *   *

It was a half hour later. Greg and Liza had taught the kids how to juggle, and now many of them had gone back to their rooms. But one little girl who had fallen in love with Cassie was telling Cassie all about the operation she'd had and holding tightly to a dog made from red balloons.

"Cassie?"

She turned around. David Silver was standing there, holding his sister Melody's hand.

Cassie had gotten so involved in entertaining the little kids that she had actually forgotten David was there.

But now he was standing right in front of her, with his little sister.

Cassie looked around, panicked. Annie was across the room talking to one of the nurses. Breezy was doing a card trick for two older kids on the table near the TV.

She was on her own. "Uh . . . hi," she managed.

"I just wanted to say what you guys did was really great," David said quietly.

"Yeah!" Melody chimed in. She was holding a pink balloon horse tightly in her right hand.

"Melody's been here for about a week. I think they're releasing her on Monday," David went on.

"That's good," Cassie said.

Silence.

Say something, Cassie ordered herself. Her

101

mind felt like a total blank. The silence seemed to go on forever.

"So . . . I'm glad you liked the show, Melody," Cassie finally added.

"It was so good!" the little girl said. "I'm naming my balloon horse Cassie, okay?"

As nervous as Cassie was, she couldn't help but smile at the adorable little girl. "That's great," she said, bending down to hug the little girl.

David smiled. "I think this is the happiest Melody's been since she's been in here."

"Can Cassie be our sister?" Melody asked her brother, her eyes wide.

Cassie blushed. David did, too. "I don't think so, Mel. I think she has a family of her own."

"I don't have any sisters," Cassie told Melody. "But if I did, I'd want her to be just like you."

"Thanks!" the little girl said, her eyes shining.

"Hey, Mel, how about if I take you back to your room?" a middle-aged nurse asked.

Melody held even more tightly to David's hand. "I want to be with my brother."

The nurse knelt down to the little girl. "How about if I escort you back, young lady, and your handsome big brother can come and see you when I get you all tucked in, okay?"

"Okay," Melody agreed reluctantly. She looked up at David. "You won't leave, will you?"

"Not a chance," David assured her.

She looked at Cassie. "Will you be my friend?"

Cassie's heart went out to the little girl. "Absolutely," she promised.

"Good," Melody said. She looked at the pink balloon horse in her hand and spoke to it. "Come on, Cassie. We have to go get back into bed now." She took the nurse's hand and obediently went off to her room.

David watched his sister leave. "Man, I hate seeing her in here. I'm really glad she's getting out soon." He turned back to Cassie. "She sure fell for you."

Cassie blushed. "She's terrific."

David smiled again. "I don't know how to thank you and your friends for what you did for her," he said shyly. "But anyway, if there's anything I can ever do for you guys, just let me know, okay?"

Well, you could fall madly in love with me, Cassie thought. *You could ask me to be your girl-friend.*

No. She could never, ever in a zillion years say anything like that.

Instead, she just said, "Okay."

David put his hands in his pockets. "So, see ya."

"See ya."

He turned and left to go see his sister.

Cassie had to find the nearest chair and sit down.

She'd finally had an actual conversation with David Silver.

And it had gone really, really, *really* well.

14

"So, what exactly did he say to you, Cassie?" Breezy eagerly demanded.

"Word for word," Annie added.

Cassie leaned back on her favorite pink polka-dotted giant pillow. It was that evening, and the girls were up in their clubhouse having a sleep-over. They were all dressed for bed. Cassie wore a pink baby doll nightie, Annie wore an oversize Cubs T-shirt, and Breezy had on a nightgown with dolphins all over it. Their sleeping bags were spread out on the floor, and they also had, close by, every kind of junk food on the planet.

Cassie smiled as she recounted exactly what David Silver had said to her that afternoon. "And then," she concluded, "he said he didn't know how to thank us for what we did for his sister, but if there was anything he could ever do for us, I should just tell him."

"Gee, Cass, you missed your chance," Annie quipped. "You could have asked him to marry you then and there."

"Very funny," Cassie said, and she threw a small pillow at Annie, which Annie neatly batted away with her head as if it were a soccer ball.

Breezy reached her hand into the giant bag of Gummi Bears and popped two into her mouth. "It's so great that you guys finally had a conversation! Now all you have to do is — "

Her sentence was interrupted by a knock at the top of the attic stairs. Breezy turned around. There was Liza, standing near the top of the stairs, rapping her knuckles on the floor. Breezy was surprised. Her sister had never, ever showed up at one of her pajama parties before.

"Hi," Breezy said.

"Hey, you guys," Liza said. "Mind if I come up for a minute?"

"No," Breezy replied eagerly. She was flattered that her grown-up sister wanted to spend time with her and her friends.

"Want some?" Annie asked, holding out a half-empty bag of chips.

"No, thanks," Liza said, sitting down with the girls.

Breezy noticed that there were dark circles under Liza's eyes, and her nails were bitten off short. That was a shocker. Liza hadn't bitten her nails since she was thirteen.

"I just wanted to thank you again for what you did at the hospital today," Liza said.

"It was no biggie," Annie replied as she chewed on some chips.

"To those little kids it was a real biggie," Liza replied. She drew her knees up and hugged them to her chin. "I can't believe Greg and I were arguing instead of doing what we were there to do."

"Greg doesn't want to call off the wedding, does he?" Cassie asked anxiously.

"No," Liza said. She bit at the nail on her pinkie.

"So . . . if you don't mind my asking, what were you fighting about, then?" Cassie asked.

Liza sighed and looked over at Breezy. "You promise you won't tell Mom?"

"We all promise not to tell anyone, right, you guys?" Breezy asked her friends. Annie and Cassie nodded in agreement.

Liza hesitated a moment, and the girls waited expectantly. "There's good news and bad news. The good news is that there's no question about us getting married."

"That's a relief," Cassie said, exhaling audibly.

"But the bad news is that Greg wants us to elope," Liza added.

"To *what*?" Cassie yelped.

"Elope," Liza repeated.

"*Elope?*" Cassie echoed. She was beyond shocked.

"You know, elope. Run off and come back married," Annie said.

"I know what it means," Cassie said. She turned to Liza. "But how could he do that to you?"

"What did you tell him?" Breezy asked her sister.

"I told him . . . I'd think about it," Liza confessed.

"Really?" Breezy asked her sister. "But why?"

Liza reached for a handful of Gummi Bears. "I'm sick of all the arguing. It's so horrible! I mean, I love Greg with all my heart. It's just not worth it."

"Yes, it is," Cassie insisted. "Your wedding day is the biggest day of your life. It *is* worth it."

Liza bit at her nail again. "Not if it's making us fight all the time," she said wearily. "Maybe the three of you are too young to understand, but — "

Another knock on the floor at the top of the stairs interrupted the conversation. This time, it was Mrs. Zeeman.

"Hi, girls, how's it going?"

"Fine," Breezy said. She wished her mom would go away. Why did she have to show up just when Liza was treating her and her friends like equals?

Mrs. Zeeman looked surprised to see Liza. "Reliving your childhood?" she asked her older daughter.

"Breezy and her friends aren't children," Liza replied.

Breezy could have hugged Liza right then. What a great sister!

"Breezy is still my little girl," Mrs. Zeeman said fondly.

"I'm not a little girl, Mom," Breezy insisted.

"I know. I just meant that you girls are growing up so fast," she added wistfully. "Anyway, Breezy, I wanted to let you know Mrs. Anders called again and asked for you. You know, about Crystal's wedding."

"That's great!" Cassie replied. "We'll have our second job!"

"Did she say when I was supposed to call her back?" Breezy asked her mom.

"She said if she wasn't home you should just keep trying," Mrs. Zeeman said, "or leave a message on her machine as to when she can reach you. But if you don't hear back from her, you should keep calling. She's not the easiest person in the world to pin down."

"Can you even imagine what a beautiful bride Crystal will be?" Cassie asked. "She's a model in Paris!"

Annie reached for the bag of Gummi Bears. "I think Liza will be the perfect bride. Models are just human clothes racks."

Liza laughed. "Thanks for the vote of confidence."

Breezy's eyes met her sister's. *I just hope you'll actually be a bride*, Breezy thought. *And that you'll have an actual wedding and not elope!*

"Liza," Mrs. Zeeman said, "could you come down to the kitchen? I need to go over the menu changes with you."

"Couldn't we do that tomorrow?" Liza asked.

"We have fifty zillion other things to do tomorrow," Mrs. Zeeman said briskly. "The caterer just faxed the new menu over. I'm glad to see they're working late for once. Come on, I'll make us some decaf." Mrs. Zeeman disappeared down the stairs.

Liza sighed and got up. "I'm starting to understand how Greg feels. Sometimes it feels more like the moms' wedding than ours."

"Maybe you should tell Mom that," Breezy suggested.

"And break her heart?" Liza asked, biting at a different nail. She took her hand out of her mouth. "Look at me! I'm biting my nails again like I did when I was a kid." She put her hands behind her back.

"If telling your mom the truth would break her heart," Cassie began hesitantly, "what do you think eloping would do?"

"You've got a point," Liza conceded. "Right now I feel like I'm being forced to choose between the guy I love and my mom. Either way, I hurt someone."

"It's you and Greg who are getting married," Annie said. "Not the moms."

"Liza!" her mother called from the bottom of the stairs. "Coffee's on!"

109

"Duty calls," Liza said. "I just don't know what the right thing to do is. I wish I did. See you guys."

"This is tragic," Cassie said, cuddling her head against one of the smaller pillows. "What if they really do elope?"

"Then ABC Weddings will be out of a job, and I'll never get my new hockey stuff."

Cassie turned on Annie. "Is that all you can think about, how much money you're going to make? I thought you wanted them to elope!"

"I've reconsidered," Annie said. "I need the bucks. Besides, who knows when we'll get our next job?"

"When I reach Mrs. Anders," Breezy said.

"*If* you ever reach Mrs. Anders," Annie corrected. She held the bag of Gummi Bears over her head and let the last three fall into her mouth.

"We should be thinking about Liza right now," Cassie said. "It would be a horrible tragedy if Liza didn't get to have her dream wedding. Don't you think so, Breezy?"

Breezy rolled over on her stomach and put her hands under her chin. She eyed the bag of potato chips, but forced herself not to take another handful. "I think Liza is so worried about not hurting Greg and not hurting the moms that she just ends up hurting herself. I've never seen her this stressed out before, ever."

"Well, if Greg would stop giving her such a hard time, she wouldn't be so stressed!" Cassie exclaimed.

Annie folded her arms. "Hey, what about what Greg wants? It's his wedding, too. Who says everything should be what the bride wants?"

"I told you before, everyone knows that when it comes to the wedding, the bride is more important than the groom — " Cassie began.

"Who says?" Annie interrupted. "That is just dumb."

"It isn't dumb," Cassie insisted.

Breezy could feel a fight coming on. Why did she always feel stuck in the middle? "You guys — "

"Now that I think about it, they really *should* just elope," Annie said. "It's just a piece of paper, anyway."

Cassie's eyes shot fire at Annie. "You can't be serious."

"I am totally serious," Annie said.

"You're only taking Greg's side because he's your brother," Cassie said.

Annie shook her head. "Wrong. I'm taking his side because he's right. Why won't Liza even compromise? I think she's acting like a spoiled brat."

Cassie swung her head to Breezy. "Did you hear what she just called your sister?"

"I think what Annie means is — "

111

"You don't have to speak for me, Breezy," Annie said heatedly. "I can speak for myself. Liza is acting like a big baby."

"Oh, and what about Greg?" Cassie shot back. "He acts like he doesn't even love her — "

"Yeah, like you know," Annie scoffed. "Just because you finally had one conversation with David Silver, you think you know all about love."

"You guys — " Breezy began again, feeling helpless.

Cassie got up and stared down at Annie. "I know more about love than you do, Annie McGee. All you do is make jokes about it. And I just don't think they're funny anymore — "

Annie stood up, too. "Because you're too busy mooning around over David Silver to think at all!"

"Who's right, Breezy?" Cassie demanded.

"Yeah, who's right?" Annie asked.

Breezy looked at her two friends, frustrated. They both stared at her, waiting for her to choose. It was a terrible position to be in. She was used to their arguing, and usually she was able to referee. But this time she didn't know what to say, because she agreed with both of them, in a way.

"What I think is this," Breezy said slowly. "I think Annie's right, because Greg and Liza are fighting so much that sometimes the whole thing really doesn't seem worth it — "

"How can you say that?" Cassie cried.

"But I also think Cassie's right, because a wedding is a very stressful thing, so people are bound to argue. And it doesn't seem to me like Greg is being very understanding about compromising, either."

"Greg is the one doing all the compromising," Annie said, her hands on her hips. She stared hard at Cassie. "All of it."

"Greg is making Liza's life miserable," Cassie shot back.

"She's the one making his life miserable!" Annie insisted.

"There's no reason for you guys to — " Breezy tried to interrupt.

Cassie glared at Annie, completely ignoring Breezy. "That is so stupid."

"Did you just call me stupid?" Annie asked, furious.

Breezy wanted to cover her head with a pillow. This was awful. She didn't know how to get them to stop fighting.

"I said what you *thought* was stupid," Cassie said sullenly.

"Fine," Annie said, looking around for her backpack. She hoisted it over her arm. "This stupid person with stupid thoughts doesn't want to spend a stupid night with her stupid friends in a stupid attic talking about stupid things. So I'm outta here."

"Annie, come on — " Breezy began. She scrambled to her feet.

113

"I'm getting dressed downstairs in the bathroom," Annie said. "I don't want to spend one more minute in the same stupid room with her."

"Annie, come on, don't leave," Breezy said.

Annie ignored her and stomped down the stairs. Since she only lived a few blocks away, both Breezy and Cassie knew she really could, and would, leave.

"I can't believe she just walked out on us!" Cassie exclaimed.

"Let's go see if we can stop her," Breezy said. "You can apologize —"

"But I don't want to apologize," Cassie said. "I wasn't wrong. She was."

Breezy felt like strangling both of them. "You were both right and wrong, okay? What difference does it make? She's our best friend!"

After a few more minutes of arguing, Breezy finally got Cassie to agree that she'd apologize if Annie would, and they headed downstairs to try and stop their friend from leaving.

But by the time they got to the front door, they saw Annie pedaling her bike toward her house.

"Annie!" Breezy called. "Please, come back! Annie!"

Either Annie didn't hear Breezy, or she didn't want to hear. With sinking hearts, Breezy and Cassie watched as Annie disappeared into the distance.

15

"**B**reezy!" her mom called up the attic stairs.

Breezy looked up from the article on dolphins she was reading in *National Geographic* magazine. "Yeah, Mom?" Breezy yelled back.

"Telephone for you!"

Breezy's heart leaped. She hoped that it would be Annie or Cassie, or maybe even both of them, calling to tell her how dumb they had been to fight, that they had made up, and that ABC Weddings was back in business. It was only ten days before Liza and Greg's wedding, and if Annie and Cassie didn't make up soon, there would be no more ABC Weddings, ever. Not even the moms would hire them again if they messed this up.

So far Breezy had had no luck at all in getting her two best friends to patch things up. It was really awful. Sure, Cassie and Annie had fought before — a lot — but this time was different. In the past, it had never been more than a day before everyone made up and forgot about the fight, and then the three of them were inseparable again.

But now, because of an argument over Liza and Greg's wedding, it looked like Cassie and Annie might never speak to each other again. Nothing Breezy said or did seemed to make any difference. Cassie was dead certain that Annie owed her an apology. Annie was just as certain that Cassie owed *her* an apology. Neither girl would budge.

So Breezy had no choice. She did things with Cassie and she did things with Annie, but the fabulous threesome was no longer. Same thing for ABC Weddings. It was a dead enterprise.

Breezy reached for the phone, full of hope.

"Hello?"

"Is this Brianna Zeeman?"

Breezy was puzzled. No one called her Brianna except for teachers on the first day of school and her grandparents.

"This is Breezy Zeeman," she said politely. "May I ask who this is?"

"This is Mrs. Abigail Anders." The woman waited expectantly, as if Breezy should know who she was.

Abigail Anders . . . Abigail Anders. Who was Abigail —

And then Breezy realized who it was. Crystal's mom! Calling at last to hire ABC Weddings to work on Crystal's wedding.

Only there *was* no ABC Weddings.

"Nice to hear from you, Mrs. Anders," Breezy said. "How's Crystal?"

"My Crystal is a high-fashion model," Mrs. Anders said proudly.

"I heard about that," Breezy said. "That's really great. When she used to baby-sit for me, she used to let me brush her hair and do all these styles on her that I tried to copy from magazines. I always thought she was so beautiful."

"Did you?" Mrs. Anders said, the delight clear in her voice. "Well, I did, too. My Crystal is a top model now. She models all over the world."

"Has she been in any of the fashion magazines?" Breezy asked eagerly.

"Oh, tons," Mrs. Anders said.

"Which ones?"

"Oh dear, I can't keep them all straight," Mrs. Anders said.

"That is so exciting," Breezy said. "Crystal is famous."

"She certainly is," Mrs. Anders agreed. "Everyone says she looks just like me."

Breezy couldn't remember if she had ever met Mrs. Anders, and if she had she certainly didn't remember what Mrs. Anders looked like. Still, she knew she should be polite. "That's really nice," she said. "And she's getting married, too."

"Yes, and that's why I'm calling," Mrs. Anders said. "I understand you have a little wedding business of your own now."

"Right," Breezy said. She decided she'd just proceed as if everything were fine with ABC Weddings. She certainly didn't want to turn down a job!

"No job is too small," Breezy added, "and your satisfaction is guaranteed."

"Wonderful. I'd like to hire you."

At last! Breezy thought happily. *Now I just have to get Annie and Cassie back to take it.*

"What do you call your little enterprise, by the way?" Mrs. Anders asked.

"ABC Weddings," Breezy replied. "It stands for Annie, Breezy, and Cassie. Annie and Cassie are my partners."

"And what sort of things do you girls do?"

"Whatever you need us to do," Breezy said. "Usually there are a lot of little things that the adults don't have time to do. We baby-sit for kids, dogs, or plants, run errands, make phone calls. Cassie knows how to do calligraphy, so we can even address the invitations."

"Very impressive," Mrs. Anders said. "I've hired Perfect Weddings, so you'd be working with your mom and Mrs. McGee on Crystal's wedding. If you're interested, that is."

"Oh, absolutely!" Breezy assured her.

"My Crystal is getting married right before Labor Day."

But that was only two weeks after Liza and Greg's wedding! Which meant that Crystal's wedding was only three and a half weeks away!

"That's kind of . . . soon, isn't it?" Breezy asked tentatively.

"It's crazy, I know," Mrs. Anders said. "But my Crystal's fiancé, Tom Logan, is a photojournalist working on a book about Russia. He leaves for Russia in September. My Crystal wants the wedding to take place before Tom leaves."

Then why didn't they start planning it sooner? Breezy wondered, but she certainly wasn't going to say anything.

"I know it's short notice," Mrs. Anders continued. "Are you too busy to take this on? I understand your sister is getting married, and frankly I had the same concern in hiring your mother — "

"It's not a problem at all," Breezy assured her quickly.

"Yes, that's just what your mother said. I'm sorry you and I played phone tag for so long. The plans for this wedding are making me nuts!"

"My mom and Mrs. McGee will change all that," Breezy said confidently. "And ABC Weddings will, too."

"Wonderful. Wait until I tell my Crystal that the little girl she baby-sat for has her own business and is working on her wedding. She'll be tickled pink!"

"Tell her I said hi," Breezy said. "I can't wait to see her."

"I'm sure she's looking forward to seeing you,

119

too, honey. She always used to say how sweet you were when she baby-sat for you. So I'll call you in a day or so, and we can have a preliminary meeting. And you can give me your rates then."

"I'd be happy to do that," Breezy said.

"I'll expect your partners to be with you at the meeting," Mrs. Anders said. "I'd like to meet all three of you."

"That's fine," Breezy replied.

"There's going to be a lot for you girls to do in a very short period of time, so I hope you are hard workers."

"Very," Breezy said firmly.

"Good. Good-bye, Brian — I mean Breezy. That's such a cute name! I'll talk to you soon."

Breezy said good-bye and put down the phone. Then she took a running leap toward a giant pillow and skidded with it across the floor. This was so exciting! ABC Weddings had just booked its second job — their first job with a nonrelative. It could lead to more jobs, and more jobs. Maybe Crystal would even recommend them to her other famous model friends, and they'd get to work on the weddings of all kinds of famous people!

"Of course, first I have to convince Cassie and Annie that they absolutely have to make up with each other," Breezy said out loud, hugging the pillow to herself. "They just have to."

She got up, took one of her grandmother's hats

from the wall, and put it on her head. Her mind was going a million miles an hour. All she had to do was to tell Cassie and Annie about this new job, and they'd see that they had to make up with each other. Getting hired by Crystal's mom was the perfect way to end their stupid fight. And if Crystal was this big model now, her wedding might turn out to be really glitzy — Cassie would love that. And it looked like they'd make a lot of money — Annie would love *that*.

So both Cassie and Annie *had* to see why their fight had to end. Didn't they?

She padded back over to the phone and quickly dialed Annie's number.

It was time to get ABC Weddings back in business.

A half hour later, Breezy's confidence had sunk to a new low. Her conversation with Annie hadn't gone at all as she had planned it. Even when she had told Annie all about her conversation with Mrs. Anders and how they had been hired to work on Crystal's wedding for *a lot of money*, Annie was not moved.

If it involved Cassie, Annie had told Breezy, they could count her out.

Now she was on the phone with Cassie, and she didn't seem to be doing any better than she had with Annie. Cassie didn't even want to *talk* about Crystal's wedding. All she wanted to do was to rehash her fight with Annie, and to discuss exactly how Breezy fit into the fight.

"So how many times have you called Annie?" Cassie asked Breezy. "Tell me honestly."

"A lot," Breezy admitted. "Just like I call you a lot, Cassie."

"So what does Annie say?"

"Cassie, come on, I don't want to be stuck in the middle — "

"All I'm asking is what Annie says."

"She says you're incredibly inconsiderate," Breezy reported.

"She's the one who's incredibly inconsiderate," Cassie replied. "You should tell her that. You should tell her — "

"Cassie . . . "

"Okay," Cassie agreed. "That isn't fair. But what Annie is doing isn't fair, either."

Breezy switched the phone to her other ear and sat on top of their hope chest. "I just don't see why you guys can't make up with each other. This is just crazy. I mean, we were just offered a huge job!"

"This is bigger than a job, Breezy," Cassie said.

"Well, then, what about how we're supposed to be best friends forever and nothing is supposed to come between us?"

"It's not my fault," Cassie insisted staunchly.

"That's just what Annie says," Breezy said, sighing. She got up to pace with the phone. "It's so nuts. Greg and Liza's wedding is on, and our perfect friendship and our great new business is off. Does that make any sense?"

"No," Cassie admitted. "And I . . . I miss us all hanging out together. And I miss ABC Weddings, too."

"Then make up with Annie!" Breezy exclaimed. "I can't ask you or Annie to do wedding stuff with me without asking the other one, too. It wouldn't be fair. And if we don't get back together, we can't accept this job."

"I guess you're right."

There was silence at the other end of the phone. Breezy felt the tiniest ray of hope. "Hey, Cassie, would you make up if Annie would make up?"

"Yes," came Cassie's small voice.

"You would? That's great! So call her and tell her!"

"She could call me, too, you know."

Breezy felt like screaming, and she knew she had to settle all this before her next conversation with Mrs. Anders.

"Will you at least think about calling her?" Breezy asked. "Please?"

"Okay, I'll *think* about it," Cassie said, clearly reluctant.

"Could you think kind of fast? Because we haven't got much time before — "

"I know, I know," Cassie interrupted. "I said

I'd think about it, and I will. Can we please change the subject now?"

"Okay," Breezy agreed. She knew she had pushed Cassie as far as she could. Well, at least now there was some hope. "So what are you doing with the rest of today?"

"Going over to the hospital to see Melody Silver," Cassie said, embarrassed. "She had to go back for a couple of days."

"How do you know about it?" And then it dawned on Breezy how Cassie would know. "Oh my gosh, David Silver called you!"

"I wish," Cassie said. "Actually, his mom stopped into the bridal shop to get a hat for her niece's wedding in Detroit. She told Mom, and Mom told me. So, what are you doing?"

"I'm going to go watch Annie's baseball game," Breezy admitted.

"Great," Cassie said, her voice cold. But then she changed the subject to something else and, a few minutes later, said good-bye.

Breezy hung up. She felt terrible. Cassie could think about calling Annie forever and never actually get around to doing it. There just had to be *something* she could do to bring the three of them back together. There was way too much at stake.

But no matter how hard she thought, she couldn't come up with a solution. Because it didn't seem like there was one at all.

16

"Cassie!" Melody cried happily when Cassie walked into her hospital room. She ran over to the older girl and gave her a huge hug.

Cassie hugged her back. "Glad to see you're all dressed."

"And I'm all ready!" Melody said eagerly.

"You look it." Cassie laughed.

Melody put her hand in Cassie's. "So, let's go!"

Since Melody was being released from the hospital that evening, her doctors had told her parents that she could be taken out of the hospital for a walk around the neighborhood that afternoon. They thought the walk would do the little girl good and help her get her strength back after her latest throat infection.

Cassie found this out when she ran into Mrs. Silver outside Melody's room. Mrs. Silver, who knew how much Melody loved Cassie, had suggested that Cassie might want to take Melody out for the walk instead of visiting with her in the room.

Mrs. Silver said she knew that Melody would be absolutely thrilled to go for a walk with Cassie — it would be much more exciting than a walk with her mom. Melody would feel like such a big girl, on her own with Cassie.

And, Mrs. Silver had told Melody with an impish grin, just to keep an eye on her baby, she'd follow and walk a discreet distance behind.

Cassie had readily agreed to the plan. And then she came up with a great idea. On an earlier visit, Cassie had told Melody all about the attic clubhouse, and she felt certain that the little girl would be thrilled to see it. Mrs. Silver thought it was a great idea, too, and Breezy's house was only a couple of blocks from the hospital. Cassie quickly called Mrs. Zeeman, who said it was fine to bring Melody over, even if Breezy was at Annie's baseball game.

On the way to Breezy's house, Melody talked a mile a minute. She pointed out her favorite birds and her favorite flowers, and even told Cassie about the boy in her class who was the nicest.

When they walked up the steps to the Zeemans' front porch, Cassie cut her eyes down to the corner of the block. Sure enough, Mrs. Silver was waiting there, standing behind a fire hydrant. Melody hadn't seen her mom at all.

"Can I ring the bell?" Melody asked.

"Sure, go ahead."

Melody rang with one hand and held tightly to Cassie with the other one.

"Now remember, Melody," Cassie said, "no one else has ever been in the clubhouse besides you, me, Annie, Breezy, and her sister, Liza."

"Does this mean I'm in the club, too?" Melody asked, wide-eyed.

"When you're twelve, which is in seven years," Cassie said, thinking quickly, "I'm sure you can be in the club, too."

"That's a very long time from now," Melody said, frowning.

"Well, how about if you're . . . an honorary little sister of the club now?" Cassie suggested.

"Yeah!" Melody agreed happily.

Mrs. Zeeman let the girls in, and Cassie led the thrilled little girl up the attic steps and into the clubhouse.

For a minute, Melody just stared at everything. Her eyes went from the pillows, to the hope chest, to the hats on the wall, to the mannequin dressed in the wedding gown.

"What do you think?" Cassie asked her.

"It's the best place I ever saw!" Melody exclaimed. She ran over to the pillow that Cassie usually used and started bouncing up and down on it as if it were a miniature trampoline.

"Lookit!" the girl called to Cassie.

"I'm lookit-ing," Cassie replied, watching as

Melody bounced off the pillow and landed on her feet, and then ran over to the dress mannequin. Next to the mannequin, Breezy had recently put up a small table her mother had found in the basement. Breezy had covered the scarred wooden table with a lacy white tablecloth. On it were the wedding veil and top hat her grandmother and grandfather had worn at their own wedding.

Melody reached out for the top hat.

"Careful," Cassie warned. "That belonged to Breezy's grandfather. He wore it at his wedding to Breezy's grandmother a long, long time ago."

"Can I touch it?" Melody asked, looking up at Cassie.

"Sure, as long as you're careful with it."

Melody lifted the top hat and put it on her head. It was so big on her that it dropped down to her chin, causing the little girl to laugh with delight. "Do I look funny?" came her muffled voice.

"Very." Cassie looked at her watch. "Melody, we have to go back soon."

Melody took off the oversize top hat, and her face fell. "I don't want to go back."

"But you're getting out of the hospital tonight," Cassie reminded the little girl.

"But I don't want to go back there at all. They give you needles."

Cassie felt badly for Melody. She tried to think of something special that might cheer her up. What would take a five-year-old's mind off going back to the hospital, to the injections that she hated?

And then she thought of it.

"Hey, Mel, there's something I want to show you," Cassie said, carefully putting the top hat back where it belonged. "Something secret."

"Super-duper secret?" Melody asked, wide-eyed. "Like on TV?"

"Even better than TV," Cassie promised. She led the little girl over to the hope chest.

"This is so pretty," Melody said, looking at the sparkly paint on the hope chest. "What is it?"

"It's called a hope chest," Cassie explained, taking the key off the chain that hung around her neck and opening the chest to give the girl a quick peek inside.

"What's it for?" Melody asked.

"You put your most precious things in it," Cassie explained. Suddenly the most terrible sadness came over her. In that chest were her, Annie's, and Breezy's most secret special hopes and dreams, dreams they hadn't shared with anyone else. But now there was no more her and Annie and Breezy. So what hope was there, really?

She felt Melody edge her tiny hand between her fingers. "Are you sad, Cassie?"

Cassie felt a huge lump in her throat. She quickly closed the chest and locked it. "I'm okay," she assured the little girl.

But really, Cassie wasn't okay at all. In fact,

she felt like crying, and she didn't know if she could stop the tears. It wasn't that she minded being the one to apologize to Annie all that much — even though she really did think that Annie was the one who was wrong. It was that deep down she had always felt like she was the third part of Breezy and Annie's being best friends. If she didn't make up with Annie, they wouldn't really miss her. And if she did apologize, the same thing would just happen again. Annie and Breezy had been best friends forever. Their moms were even best friends, while Mrs. Zeeman and Mrs. McGee barely even knew her mother.

Three really wasn't a very good number for best friends at all.

Cassie felt one tear slide out of her eye, and she quickly turned away from Melody and fisted the tear from her cheek. She certainly didn't want Melody to see her cry. The little girl had enough sad things to think about without having to worry about Cassie. She would just have to compose herself. Maybe if she splashed some cold water on her face. If she could be alone for just a minute . . .

"Melody," Cassie said, "I have to run downstairs to the bathroom, and then I need to take you back to your mom. If I leave you here for a minute, will you be okay?"

"Sure." Melody wandered back over to the top hat and wedding veil.

Cassie hurried down the stairs to the second-floor bathroom, leaving the little girl behind.

So she never saw when Melody went back over to the hope chest.

She never saw when Melody tried to lift up the lid of the chest.

And she never saw that although she *thought* she had locked the hope chest, she hadn't firmly clasped the lock. So she never saw the little girl get the hope chest open and peer inside.

Inside the hope chest, Melody was shocked to see a photograph of her very own big brother. That was pretty weird. What was a picture of her brother doing in there? Melody stuck the photograph in her pocket. Then she noticed a piece of paper with a lot of writing on it, most of which she couldn't read. But she already knew her letters, and although she didn't know what P-R-I-N-C-E spelled, she recognized her brother's name when she saw it, after those P-R-I-N-C-E letters.

She stuck the piece of paper in her pocket, too.

Then she closed the hope chest, and it locked.

When Cassie came back from the bathroom, Melody was once again playing with the bridal veil and top hat. She never said a word about the things she had taken out of the hope chest.

So Cassie had no idea at all that they were gone.

17

Two days later, Cassie stood at the door of David and Melody Silver's house, her heart pounding. When she'd called Mrs. Silver to ask whether she could come over to see Melody, Mrs. Silver had told her that Melody would be thrilled to see her, that the little girl talked about Cassie all the time.

Cassie told herself that visiting Melody had nothing to do with Melody's big brother. Not that she succeeded, but she tried her best not to even wonder if David was home.

And she had to fill her time up with something. She and Annie were still not speaking to each other. At least twice a day, Cassie started to pick up the phone to call Annie, but every time something made her stop herself.

Deep down, Cassie wanted Annie to prove that she cared enough about Cassie to pick up the phone and call her. Even if it was silly, that was how she felt. It wasn't any fun to always feel like you were the one who cared more than the other person.

Cassie was sure Annie wasn't lying in bed at night worrying about their friendship like she was. She was sure Annie wasn't giving the whole thing any thought at all. Well, Cassie vowed that she wouldn't, either. And things weren't so bad. Breezy was still her best friend, even if she did have to share Breezy with Annie. And she was still going to Liza and Greg's wedding, and it would still be magical. She would just ignore Annie through the entire wedding if she had to.

She just wished she didn't have to.

Cassie rang the doorbell with her right hand, as her left hand held a huge bunch of red helium balloons she'd picked up. She knew how much Melody loved balloons.

David Silver answered the door.

Cassie gulped.

"Hi, uh, David," she squeaked.

I squeaked! Cassie thought in a panic. *I actually squeaked!*

"Hi," he said. "Melody told me you were coming over to see her."

"That's why I came," Cassie said, feeling like an idiot. "To see her."

"Yeah, I just said that." David let her into the house. Walking behind him, Cassie hit herself on the head. *Get a grip,* she ordered herself. *You have a brain. He's just a boy. Just the per-*

fect boy. Just the most wonderful, perfect, sweet, smart —

"Hey, you brought Melody balloons," David said, turning back to Cassie.

Her face turned the same color as the balloons in her hand. *Stop it*, she told herself. *He doesn't know what you were thinking. Remember what Annie and Breezy told you — just be yourself.*

"Right, balloons," Cassie said, trying to sound like herself — whatever *that* meant. "Melody loves balloons. So I brought her some. Balloons."

"Yeah. I see that." David put his hands in his jean pockets. "How come you're so nice to her?"

"Well, because she's terrific," Cassie replied.

There, Cassie thought with relief. *That was better. That was a normal sentence.*

"She told me yesterday she wants to grow up to be just like you," David confided.

"Oh, well, we don't even have the same color hair," Cassie joked. David didn't smile. "I mean, not that hair color is important. Because it isn't."

"I think she meant on the *inside*," David pointed out.

Cassie bit her lower lip. "Right. I knew that."

She tried to smile at David, but her face wasn't working right. Desperately, she wished she could go back out to the porch and start this whole thing over again. Why did David have to answer the door? If only she'd known ahead of time, she could have been prepared!

"Cassie!" Melody cried, running down the hallway and dodging around her brother to jump into Cassie's arms. "I'm all better!"

Cassie instantly felt more at ease now that Melody was there. "I can see that," she said, laughing. Why couldn't she talk to David as easily as she could talk to his little sister? "I brought some — "

"Balloons!" Melody shrieked with joy, reaching up for the balloons in Cassie's hand. "Hooray! Come see my room, okay?"

"She seems like she's feeling better," Cassie said to David as Melody began to drag her toward her room.

"A certain girl she worships really helped with that," David said.

Cassie followed David and Melody upstairs and into a very girly-looking room. Melody's room had pink wallpaper with silver stars and hearts on it, and her bed was covered with stuffed animals and dolls.

"This one's my favorite!" Melody said as she thrust a small stuffed zebra at Cassie.

"What's its name?" Cassie asked.

"Her name is Cassie," Melody said proudly.

"And how about that stuffed panda bear?" Cassie asked.

"That's Cassie, too."

"And the doll with the frilly dress?" Cassie asked.

"Cassie," the little girl said. "I even named all my Barbie dolls Cassie!"

"See, she really does worship you," David said from the doorway.

Cassie sat on Melody's bed and hugged the little girl. "I'm very honored."

"What's honored mean?"

"It means that it makes me happy that you like me enough to name your special stuffed animals and your dolls after me."

"Oh." Melody thought for a minute. "Well, I'm honored that you're honored!"

Cassie and David both laughed, which made Melody laugh, too.

"Hey, watch this," the little girl said eagerly. "Betcha I can make it fly!" She tried to tie a helium balloon to the giraffe named Cassie. Cassie helped, but the giraffe was too heavy. "It doesn't work," Melody said, clearly disappointed.

David went over and took five balloons from his sister. Then he sat down on the bed next to Cassie and quickly tied the balloons to the legs and the neck of the stuffed giraffe.

It floated upside down to the ceiling, and the little girl was so happy that she actually danced and giggled at the same time.

"It's flying! It's flying!" Melody squealed.

Cassie couldn't believe it. She was at David Silver's *house*. He was sitting on the bed *right next to her*. They had actually spent *the last fifteen minutes together.*

The next thought that popped into her brain was: *I have to tell Breezy and Annie right away!*

But there was no more Breezy and Annie. Not together, anyway. Not together with her.

The same old lump came to Cassie's throat. It was one thing to vow not to care, but it was another thing to get your heart to actually roll over and play dead.

18

"**S**o you see, Cassie, it's a total emergency!"
"You want me to come over, Breezy, and help you look?"

"You have to!" Breezy said emphatically. "I can't believe I lost it."

"I'll help you find it, I promise," Cassie assured her. "I'll be over right away."

"Thanks. You're the best, Cassie."

Breezy hung up the phone and smiled. This time her plan was going to work. It just had to.

It was two days later, two days closer to Greg and Liza's wedding. And still Cassie and Annie weren't speaking to each other. All they did was complain noisily to Breezy about each other.

Finally, Breezy couldn't take it anymore. She knew she had to do something to bring them together. Both their friendship and their business depended on it.

On top of that, the clock was ticking. That very evening, Breezy was supposed to have a conference with Mrs. Anders about Crystal's wedding, and Mrs. Anders was expecting her to bring her partners. Only at the moment she didn't *have* any partners.

She had to come up with some plan, and she had to come up with it quickly.

And then it hit her. Of course. What they needed was a common purpose! It had to be something that would get both Annie and Cassie involved, something that had nothing to do with ABC Weddings.

So what if, accidentally of course, she were to take the chain that held her key to the hope chest off her neck? And what if, just as accidentally, the chain and key disappeared? Who would be the logical person for her to call, if she were frantic, to help her look for it?

Breezy smiled. It was foolproof.

Unless, of course, either friend asked if she was calling the other friend.

She got on the phone and put her plan into action.

Cassie promised to come over right away. Ten minutes before, Annie had promised exactly the same thing.

And both girls were so worried about how frantic Breezy was that neither asked anything at all about the other one.

Annie and Cassie showed up within a minute of each other. When they found Breezy up in the clubhouse, the first thing they both noticed was that Breezy's key was hanging around her neck. She hadn't really lost it at all.

"You tricked us," Annie accused.

"I know," Breezy said. "And I'm glad it worked, too. Are you guys mad?"

Cassie looked sideways at Annie, who looked sideways back at her. "I'm not if she's not," Annie said.

Cassie nodded, her eyes on the floor.

Breezy hadn't realized she was holding her breath, but now she exhaled with relief. It was clear to her that both of her friends were just looking for some excuse to mend their friendship, since neither one of them was mad at her.

"You guys," Breezy began earnestly, "just because we're best friends doesn't mean we have to agree about everything, you know? Our friendship is stronger than that. Isn't it?"

Annie and Cassie both slowly nodded their heads in agreement.

"Good," Breezy said, grinning. "Let's just forget all about the fight, okay?"

"If she apologizes to me first," Annie said, leaning against the wall.

"If she apologizes to me first," Cassie stated, leaning against the other wall.

Cassie and Annie looked down at the floor. "I'm sorry," each of them said, very sincerely, at exactly the same time.

Then they both looked up at each other and cracked up at the same time.

Breezy threw one of the smaller pillows into the air. "I'm *so* glad that's over!"

"I feel much better!" Cassie admitted, plopping down next to Breezy.

"Me too," Annie admitted. She pulled her baseball cap out of the back pocket of her jeans and put it low on her head, covering her eyes. "To tell you guys the truth, I kinda . . . really missed the three of us."

Cassie's mouth fell open with surprise. "You did?"

"Yeah," Annie said. "I kept thinking that you probably didn't care that much — "

"That's what I thought about you," Cassie exclaimed. "Wow, I feel so much better now."

"Me too," Annie said.

"Me three!" Breezy chimed in. "Listen, I've got to tell the two of you about this meeting we're supposed to go to with Mrs. Anders. It's tonight, and we're supposed to give her an estimate, and — "

"Time-out," Annie said, making a T-shape with her hands. "There's something else I think we should do first."

"What?" Cassie asked.

Annie got up and went over to the hope chest. She held out her hands. Breezy and Cassie got up and joined her, each taking a hand so that they

141

formed a triangle, the hope chest in the center.

Annie looked at Breezy and then at Cassie, her face solemn. "I think we need to open the hope chest, and each of us needs to put something new in it."

"Right," Cassie agreed. "And pledge that we'll never, ever, ever fight like this again."

"Right," Annie said. "We shouldn't get all bent out of shape just because we each have minds of our own."

"And today we make a solemn vow to remember that forever, at all times," Cassie said. "What should we put in the hope chest?"

"Anything we have on us," Breezy said. "Because it will be the thought that counts."

Simultaneously, the three girls reached into their pockets. Annie pulled out her ever-present Nerf ball. Cassie found a red balloon. And Breezy took out the tiny metal dolphin that she carried around for good luck.

"Cool," Annie said. "Breezy, since you were the one who brought us all back together, you should open the hope chest."

Breezy was so happy! Greg and Liza hadn't eloped, and the wedding was going on as planned, and ABC Weddings was going to work on their wedding and Crystal Anders's wedding.

But most important of all, the fabulous three-some was back together again.

She took the key from around her neck, leaned

over, and opened the hope chest so they could each put their stuff into it. They each looked down into it.

Breezy's dolphin in its glass dome was right there.

Annie's photo of the flyer Amelia Earhart was there, too. And Greg and Liza's photo.

But Cassie's photo of David Silver and the short story she had written about Prince David and Princess Cassie were nowhere to be seen.

All three girls stared into the chest in disbelief. For a long time, no one said anything.

Then, finally, Cassie looked at Annie. Her face was pale and there were tears on her eyelashes. "You!" she said, pointing at Annie. "You stole it."

"What are you talking about?" Annie asked.

"You stole my stuff from the hope chest!"

"I did not!" Annie said self-righteously. "I never — "

"You did too," Cassie said, wiping the tears from her cheeks. "Breezy would never take those things. And you're the only other person with a key."

Annie put her hands on her hips. "Cassie, why would I take your stuff?"

"So you could laugh about it," Cassie said, her tears spilling over again. "You didn't really miss our threesome at all. You only made up with me so you could laugh at me. Cassie is such a big joke. She has such a big crush on David Silver that she put his picture in the hope chest — "

"Cassie, I didn't take — "

"You're a liar!" Cassie shouted. "I can't believe I actually fell for this. You were never really going to make up with me. You just wanted to humiliate me, isn't that right?"

"No," Annie said. She turned to Breezy. "Tell her I would never do that!"

"I . . . I . . . " Breezy stammered. She didn't know what to think or who to believe. This was an absolute disaster!

"Who did you show my story to, Annie?" Cassie demanded, tears streaming down her face. "How many more people are laughing at me?"

"No one!" Annie insisted, throwing her hands in the air. "I didn't take your stupid stuff, Cassie!"

"I really hate you, Annie!" Cassie ran sobbing from the attic.

Breezy looked at Annie. "Did you take it?"

"What, you don't believe me either?" Annie asked, her voice rising.

"Annie, no one else has a key."

"So that makes me suspect number one?" Annie asked. "You think that's fair?"

"I don't know what to think," Breezy said, sighing. She shook her head. "This is so awful."

Annie walked over to Breezy and looked her in the eye. "I thought you knew me better than this," she said. "But if it makes you feel better . . . I swear to you, Breezer, I have not opened the hope chest since the last time the three of us opened it together."

"I heard that!" Cassie screamed at Annie from the stairs. "You're a liar, Annie!"

"Great, fine," Annie said, throwing her hands into the air. "I thought you two were my best friends. But if you both believe I'm a liar and a cheat, then I guess I thought wrong."

Annie ran down the stairs past Cassie and headed for the front door.

She got on her bike and pedaled toward home. And for the first time in she couldn't remember how long, tough Annie McGee found herself crying.

19

"What do you think of this one?" Mrs. Anders asked, turning to the next page in Crystal's portfolio book and pointing to an advertisement torn from a newspaper for a back porch swing. Crystal was sitting on the swing, drinking something from a tall, clear glass.

Breezy was sitting with Mrs. Anders in her living room, looking over Mrs. Anders's shoulder at yet another picture of Crystal. As far as Breezy could see, Crystal didn't look all that different from how she had looked when she'd been Breezy's baby-sitter. Her hair was blonder, and it was now cut into a chin-length bob, but other than that she looked pretty much the same. Cute. Really cute. But short.

Breezy couldn't figure that out. She had always thought that models had to be really tall. Unless Crystal had grown a whole lot, Breezy didn't think she could be more than five-four.

Not that she'd ever say anything to Mrs. Anders. And maybe some models were short, and Breezy just didn't know about it.

"Very nice," Breezy said, trying to look as if she really were interested.

Mrs. Anders turned the page. "Oh, this is one of my favorites. Doesn't my Crystal look gorgeous here?"

It was another page torn from a newspaper. This time Crystal was wearing a white bikini and sitting in a hot tub with a cute guy. The ad said in big letters that it was the last chance to get the hot tub for 25 percent off.

"Wow," Breezy said, trying to sound enthusiastic.

Breezy snuck a peek at her watch. Mrs. Anders had been slowly going through Crystal's portfolio with her for the past twenty minutes. Breezy was trying her best to be polite, especially since she knew she had promised to have her partners with her for this meeting, and her partners had decided only a few hours earlier that they hated each other's guts.

Maybe I should have canceled this appointment, Breezy worried for the hundredth time. *I feel kind of dishonest not telling Mrs. Anders the truth — that there is no ABC Weddings, and that I doubt very much that there ever will be.*

But maybe I can work on Crystal's wedding by myself.

Or maybe some miracle will happen and Annie and Cassie will make up.

No way, Breezy thought.

"Oh, this one is so sweet, don't you think?" Mrs. Anders asked, turning to still another page of what seemed to be an endless portfolio of advertisements starring Crystal. This one was for a lawn care company. Crystal was riding on the back of a power mower. She was dressed in overalls with a daisy in her hair.

"Cute," Breezy said.

"What time did you say your partners would be here?" Mrs. Anders asked.

"Uh . . . " Breezy began. She didn't want to lie. But she didn't want to lose the job, either. Maybe Mrs. Anders would decide she'd be willing to go ahead without her partners.

"Hey, I'd love to see Crystal's other portfolio!" she said brightly.

"What do you mean?"

"Well, this one is all newspaper ads for products," Breezy said. "And you said she had done all these fashion magazine jobs. I'd love to see that."

Mrs. Anders shut the portfolio hastily. "Oh, there's just too many. My Crystal models with all the supermodels, you know."

"That must be really exciting."

"Oh, yes," Mrs. Anders agreed. "I was a model once, too, you know. I probably still could. I look much younger than my age — everyone says so."

Breezy didn't have a clue what to say to that. She smiled, but inside she felt defeated. Sooner or later she was going to have to tell Mrs. Anders the truth, she could see that now. There really wasn't any way to get around it.

"Mrs. Anders . . . about my partners —"

"They're awfully late, aren't they," Mrs. Anders said, looking at her watch.

"They . . . I . . . " Breezy knew she should tell the truth. But she just couldn't.

She took a deep breath. "I should have told you sooner, Mrs. Anders. But they couldn't make it to this meeting."

Mrs. Anders's eyebrows shot up. "Why?"

"They . . . had to do . . . something else," Breezy said lamely. "I mean, it was planned before this meeting was planned. But they trust me to handle the negotiations."

Mrs. Anders studied Breezy. "There's something about you that makes me trust you, young lady. Besides, I'm absolutely frantic trying to get this wedding together so quickly. So I'm going to take your word for it. All right. But I expect your partners to be at every other meeting, Brianna. I'm hiring three girls and I expect to see three girls."

"Yes, ma'am," Breezy agreed. "No problem."

"So, let's talk details. I'm sure you'll want to take notes," Mrs. Anders said.

149

Breezy had already planned on taking notes, and she pulled her notebook and pen out of her backpack. Mrs. Anders launched into a fifteen-minute monologue about how the wedding was going to take place at Summerville Methodist Church, and the party was going to be at one of the fanciest French restaurants in Indianapolis, and then the after-party party was going to be under a tent in the Anders's backyard, and how much fun the whole thing was going to be, and how utterly perfect both she and her Crystal were going to look.

When she took a breath, Breezy looked up from her notes. She knew a lot about the wedding now. But she didn't have a clue as to what ABC Weddings was supposed to do.

"The wedding sounds wonderful," Breezy said. "But I can't really give you an estimate until you tell me what it is you want ABC Weddings to do."

"Oh, all the little odds and ends," Mrs. Anders said, waving her hand airily.

"But if you could be more specific, it would help me to — "

The grandfather clock in the Anders's family room chimed eight o'clock, which threw Mrs. Anders into a panic. She jumped up from the couch. "I can't believe how late it is!"

Breezy got up, too. "But Mrs. Anders, I still — "

"I know it's here somewhere," Mrs. Anders murmured, rummaging through the back of Crystal's portfolio. "Ah! Here it is. This is ABC Weddings's contract with me. I promise to keep you girls hopping! There's probably enough work for six girls, so I hope the three of you are fast-fast-fast!"

Breezy felt terrible that she had lied to Crystal's mom. This time she really didn't think she could get Annie and Cassie to make up. If Mrs. Anders had a lot of work for three girls, there was no way one girl could do it all by herself. Not even a girl who worked as hard as Breezy worked.

She was just going to have to tell the truth. Even if it meant losing the job.

"About my partners, Mrs. Anders — " Breezy began.

"No time, no time," Mrs. Anders said, handing Breezy her backpack. She ushered Breezy to the front door. "Just fill in the contract with the amount ABC Weddings will charge per hour, let your mom review it, and then just mail it to me. You biked over here, right? Good, then you have your bike outside. Forgive me, but I am so late for a bridge date and I haven't even put my face on yet!"

"But Mrs. Anders, there's something I have to — "

"Bye, Brianna!" Mrs. Anders called, as she practically pushed Breezy out the door. "Get it back to me by the weekend!"

Then Mrs. Anders shut the door and Breezy was left standing on the front porch holding a contract she was supposed to fill in for a business with partners that didn't exist.

She trudged wearily over to her bike and unlocked the lock that held it to a small birch tree. She got on and began to pedal toward home.

Dusk was beginning to fall, and down the street the last game of stickball was breaking up for the evening. Breezy wished she had something simple to think about, like a stickball game, instead of all the problems that were going around and around in her head.

She couldn't go over Mrs. Anders's contract with her mom without telling her mom the truth about Annie and Cassie. Breezy was pretty sure Annie hadn't told her own mother, since Annie tended not to tell her mother anything important — her mother just got too stressed out over everything.

Which meant Breezy was going to have to break the bad news to the partners of Perfect Weddings.

Annie and Cassie and Breezy were no longer best friends. And this time Breezy was pretty sure they never would be again. One of them had stolen something precious from the other. One of them had lied about it. How could you just get over something like that?

How could you?

20

Breezy lay on her back in the attic clubhouse, staring up at the ceiling. How had everything gone so hideously wrong?

Since the big fight between Annie and Cassie, nothing Breezy had said or done had accomplished even a little to fix things. It was horrible. Cassie was certain that Annie had betrayed her. But Annie swore that she was innocent.

Breezy was so sad. She didn't know who or what to believe. She didn't think that Annie would ever do something like that. On the other hand, David Silver's photo and Cassie's short story about him really *were* missing.

So maybe Annie had done it. And now she was lying to cover up.

But if that was true, then Annie wasn't the person Breezy thought she was.

That possibility made Breezy even sadder. And the fact that they'd been offered a big job by Mrs. Anders, which Breezy had been unable to turn

153

down even though she knew she should have, made her feel even sadder than that. On top of that, she was really disappointed in herself for lying to Mrs. Anders.

Sooner or later she was going to have to tell her mother everything. Probably sooner. That morning at breakfast, her mother had told her that Mrs. Anders had called again, asking when she would get ABC Weddings's contract back. Breezy had mumbled some lame excuse and fled up to the attic. Postponing the inevitable wasn't going to fix anything.

Breezy sat up and stared forlornly at the hope chest. Once it had been the most magical, special thing inside their most magical, special clubhouse. But now when Breezy looked at the chest, she felt even sadder than she'd felt before.

"I just have to talk to someone about all this, someone other than Mom," Breezy said out loud, even though there was no one there to hear her.

Then she thought of Liza. Hadn't Liza shared her secret problems with Breezy? Didn't they have a new kind of relationship where Liza didn't think of Breezy as just a little kid? Yes, confiding in Liza made perfect sense, even if it was only a few days before Liza's wedding. Liza and Greg hadn't had a fight in days, and all the wedding plans were going smoothly now. And maybe hearing about Breezy's problem would help Liza get her mind off of her pre-wedding jitters.

Quickly, Breezy got up and went downstairs to Liza's room. The door was shut. Breezy knocked. No answer. That was funny. She could have sworn that Liza had said she'd be in her room taking a nap because she had a headache.

Breezy knocked again. "Liza? It's me."

Still no answer. Breezy pushed just a little on the door and peered inside.

The room was empty.

She pushed the door open a notch further. Liza's closet was wide open, and there were a few hangers on the floor, but other than that, everything looked normal. And yet Breezy got this weird feeling that something about the room wasn't right.

But what was it?

At that moment, she knew.

Liza kept her suitcase on the floor of her closet. Since the closet was open, Breezy could see inside.

No suitcase.

Breezy pushed through the door and rushed over to the closet. Liza's favorite clothes were missing. Where could she have gone?

Trying not to panic, Breezy whirled around, her eyes scanning the room for some kind of clue as to where Liza could have gone. She rushed over to the nightstand next to the bed and saw some notes scribbled on a pad of paper.

"Southwest Air, Reno, Flight 555," the note

read, followed by that day's date and the time of the flight — three-fifteen.

A terrible feeling came over Breezy as the truth dawned on her. She sat heavily on Liza's bed.

Breezy had heard that you can get married really quickly in the state of Nevada, and Reno was in Nevada.

Liza and Greg were eloping.

Not only that, they were eloping that very day. In fact, their flight was departing in just a few hours. Next to the notepad was a letter that Liza had started to their mom. Breezy felt guilty reading it but she read it anyway.

Dear Mom,

Please don't hate me for running away to elope. It isn't what I want. But I can't go on fighting with Greg. I love him too much. I'll find some way to pay you back for all the money you and Dad have spent. I know I'm breaking your heart, which breaks my heart. And I guess I'll just have to live without having the wedding I've always dreamed of. But I love Greg and

Here the letter stopped. And to Breezy, it looked as if falling tears had blurred the last two words Liza had written.

Breezy was so shocked she couldn't move. She felt terrible. Liza didn't really want to elope —

156

she had said as much in her letter. On top of that, Breezy knew the moms would be heartbroken. In fact, *she* felt heartbroken.

But what could she do about it?

Something. She had to do something. And she knew she couldn't do it by herself.

Finally an idea came to her. It was a long shot, but it was worth a try.

Quickly she picked up the phone and dialed Annie's number. "Please be home, please be home," she chanted to herself as the phone rang. "I can't do this without you and Cassie."

Breezy paced as the phone rang, praying that her two best friends would help her, and that if they did, the three of them wouldn't be too late.

"You told me that you weren't calling Cassie," Annie said sourly as she came into the clubhouse a half hour later and saw Cassie there.

"Well, she told me she wasn't calling you, either," Cassie told Annie. She had arrived at Breezy's just five minutes earlier.

"Okay, I lied," Breezy admitted. "Again. But it was for a good cause."

"I can't believe I fell for this twice," Annie said with disgust. She headed for the stairs.

"Me neither," Cassie said, right behind her on the stairs.

"Wait, you guys!" Breezy called to them. "Look, I'm sorry I had to lie to get you both here, but this time there really is an emergency. I didn't lie about that!"

Both girls turned back to her.

"How do we know that isn't a lie, too?" Annie asked.

"Yeah, Annie would know," Cassie added. "She's the best liar I ever met."

"That's it, I'm outta here," Annie said, turning around.

"Me too," Cassie said.

Breezy couldn't take it anymore. "If you both want to be that selfish, go ahead," she yelled down the stairs to her friends. "My sister is in a terrible crisis and she needs our help. But all you two ever think about anymore is yourselves and your stupid fight!"

Cassie and Annie both stopped at the bottom of the stairs and looked back up at Breezy.

"You yelled," Cassie marveled, staring up at her. "You never yell."

"I'm upset, okay?" Breezy replied. "Everything is a mess. This summer was supposed to be so great, but every single thing that could go wrong has gone wrong. And now the most horrible thing of all is about to happen. Not that the two of you care." She went to her favorite pillow and sank down on it, burying her head in her hands.

Faintly she heard Cassie's sandals and Annie's sneakers trudging back up the stairs. They sat next to her.

She lifted her head and looked at them.

"We might be mad at each other, but we're not mad at you," Cassie said softly.

"So tell us what's wrong," Annie added.

Quickly Breezy filled her friends in on the notepad with the airline flight information she had found in Liza's room.

"Oh my gosh, you mean they're really eloping?" Cassie asked.

"It sure looks like it to me," Breezy said.

Cassie looked over at Annie. "I suppose you're going to gloat about this."

"You suppose wrong, Cassie," Annie said quietly. "For one thing, my mom will be really, really hurt. And I don't think it's right for Liza and Greg to just run away like this, not with the wedding on Sunday."

"Liza didn't want to do it," Breezy said. "I'm sure of it." She pulled out the letter Liza had started and showed it to her friends.

"This is so terrible!" Cassie cried, tears in her eyes. "We have to do something!"

Annie folded her arms. "I don't see that there's anything we can do. And even if there was something we could do, I wouldn't do it with a *former* friend who thinks I'm a big liar."

"Oh, I suppose my story and the photo of David just grew wings and flew out of the hope chest by themselves," Cassie said.

Annie gave Cassie a cold look. "Maybe you took

it out yourself so you could make me look bad in front of Breezy. How do I know?"

Cassie's jaw dropped in disbelief. "I would never ever do a thing like that!"

"Well, I wouldn't take your stuff and then lie about it!" Annie shot back.

Breezy scrambled to her feet. "Forget it, you guys! Just forget it! I can't stand this anymore. I'll figure out some way to help Liza by myself —"

"I'll help you," Cassie assured her, getting to her feet.

"So will I," Annie said, getting up.

"I thought you wouldn't be involved in anything if I was in it," Cassie reminded her.

"For the last time, this isn't about the two of you!" Breezy cried. "I don't know who did what, and right now I don't even care. This is about Liza and Greg. Now, are we going to try and do something, or are the two of you too busy fighting to think about anyone but yourselves?"

Annie's eyes stayed hard, but Cassie nodded. "You're right, Breezy. Unlike *someone* I know, I care about true love. I'll help."

"Not so fast," Annie piped up. "I'm . . . I'm helping, too. Even if Cassie is involved."

"Good," Breezy said, sighing with relief. "Now, I think I've figured out a plan. It's a long shot, but —"

"What is it?" Annie asked.

"What do we do?" Cassie added.

"I'll tell you everything," Breezy said, looking at her watch. "And we have to do it quickly, or it will be too late. The first step is . . ."

"Is what?" Cassie prompted.

"The first step is," Breezy repeated, "we call David Silver."

21

As the taxi driver turned the corner onto David Silver's street, Breezy clutched the twenty-dollar bill she'd unpinned from her grandmother's mannequin tightly in her hand.

It somehow seemed right to her that the first twenty dollars she had ever made from ABC Weddings was about to be used to pay for a taxi to the airport, where ABC Weddings, together again in name if not in spirit, was going to try to stop Liza and Greg from eloping.

Breezy looked over at Annie and Cassie, who sat next to her. Cassie's golden skin was ashen. Annie's mouth was clenched tight. The two of them had not said two words to each other since they'd gotten into the cab. But at least they were both there. And they each had told Breezy privately that they were ready to contribute their own twenty dollars to pay for the cab, if it was needed.

"I can't believe David actually said yes to this," Cassie said nervously, biting her lower lip.

"It's at the end of the block," Breezy told the driver, "the last house on the right."

She turned to Cassie. "I guess David Silver meant it when he told you he wanted to repay you for being so nice to his little sister."

"I really like Melody," Cassie said. "I wasn't being nice to her because of David."

"Yeah, right," Annie snorted under her breath. "I believe that."

Cassie gave her a sharp look. "I'm not like that. Maybe *you* are, but — "

"You guys quit it. Either we're a team, or let's just forget it and go home," Breezy said impatiently as the cab driver pulled into David's driveway. "Agreed?"

"Agreed," Cassie mumbled, while Annie just nodded.

"Oh, my gosh, there he is," Cassie said as David, his best friend, Ben, and David's little sister came out the front door. Cassie slunk down low in her seat.

"I know David said he was bringing Ben," Annie said, "but what's with Melody?"

"Hi," David said, sticking his head into the open window of the taxi. "My parents aren't home and I couldn't find a sitter for the squirt, so — "

"Hi, Cassie!" Melody cried happily.

"Hi," Cassie managed. "Hi, Ben. Hi, David," she added shyly.

"So, is it okay?" David asked.

"I get to come!" Melody chortled.

"Lucky for you this is a station wagon," the taxi driver said. "Climb in. Round-trip to the airport, right? Sheesh, my boss will kill me for taking you kids. How old is that little one, anyway?"

"I'm her brother. I'll be responsible for her," David assured the driver as they got into the car.

"You kids got money to pay for this?" the driver asked dubiously.

"Yes, sir," Breezy said. She showed him her twenty-dollar bill.

"And there's more where that came from," Annie added, trying to sound adult and confident.

"Never tell strangers you've got money," the driver admonished them. "People get robbed that way!"

"But you just asked if we — " Annie began.

"Just everybody do up your seat belts and let's get this show on the road," the driver said, turning back around.

With Melody and David in the very back, Ben in the front seat, and the girls in the middle, the driver took off for the airport.

"It's really nice of you guys to help us," Breezy told David and Ben.

Ben shrugged. "If it was up to me — "

"Yeah, but it wasn't," David said. "I dusted you

at basketball, so I got to pick what we'd do today. That was the deal we made."

"Yeah, well, I hope no one who knows me is at the airport," Ben mumbled.

"I told you," David said, "you don't have to do anything. All you have to do is stand there. I'll do it all."

"You're gonna look like a jerk," Ben said, poking his friend in the ribs.

"I'll worry about that," David replied.

"Don't say my big brother looks like a jerk," Melody insisted, scowling. "*You're* a jerk!"

"Man, I'm sure glad I don't have a little sister," Ben muttered.

Gathering up all her nerve, Cassie turned around and smiled at David. "Thanks," she said. "I mean it."

David smiled back at her. "You're welcome."

As the taxi driver got onto the interstate and headed south toward the airport, Breezy nervously looked at her watch again. The traffic was bad, and Liza and Greg's plane was scheduled to take off in an hour and thirty minutes.

"Can't you go any faster?" Breezy pleaded with the driver.

"Sorry," the cabdriver said, looking at Breezy in his rearview mirror. "Traffic is traffic, kid. I can't fly over 'em."

"Hey, are we going on an airplane?" Melody asked, bouncing up and down with excitement.

"No, we're just going to the airport," her brother told her.

"What for?" Melody asked, confused.

"To try and keep two people from making a huge mistake," Cassie explained. "I just hope we aren't too late."

Come on, come on, come on, Breezy chanted inside her head as their taxi inched its way along the service road to the airport. Even here the traffic was terrible. It seemed as if everyone in Indianapolis needed to get to the airport at the exact same time. She looked at her watch for what seemed like the zillionth time. Greg and Liza's flight was scheduled to depart in twenty minutes. In fact, if the flight was on time, Breezy was pretty sure it was probably boarding already.

"Man, this traffic is something else, huh?" the driver said, popping a stick of gum in his mouth. They were at a total standstill.

"You guys, let's get out," Breezy said impetuously. "We can get there faster if we run."

"Hey!" the driver objected. "You're just kids. You can't go running around without an adult — "

Breezy didn't listen. She smacked her twenty-dollar bill into his palm, picked up her backpack, and opened the door, not even waiting for change.

"Be careful! Stay out of traffic!" the driver called to them as they carefully crossed to the walkway that led to the airport. "I'm waiting for

166

you at the taxi stand!" the driver called after them. "Hey, you hear me? I feel kinda responsible for you kids now!"

The group ran as fast as they could, knowing that every second mattered now. David had Melody in his arms. She thought the whole thing was a blast.

"Faster, Davey, faster!" she squealed happily.

"Man, you weigh a ton," David groaned, trying to keep up with everyone else with Melody in his arms. "What have you been eating?"

"This way!" Annie said as she spotted the sign that indicated the way to the gates.

The five of them ran down Concourse B, pausing only to go through the metal detectors, which seemed to take forever.

"Which gate are we looking for?" Cassie asked breathlessly.

"We have to check," Breezy said, stopping in front of a large computerized sign that listed the various airline arrivals and departures. She looked down at the flight information on the scrap of paper she'd torn from the pad on Liza's nightstand and scanned the sign until she found the right flight.

"Gate nine," she said when she finally found it. "Let's go! They're boarding. It's on time."

The group all started running toward Gate 9 as fast as they could.

"This is the final boarding call for Southwest

Air Flight five-five-five to Reno," came a melodious voice over the intercom system. "Final boarding."

"That's their flight!" Cassie cried as they all started to run even faster.

"Please don't let us be too late, please," Breezy said under her breath.

"What if they're already on the plane?" Cassie asked.

No one had an answer.

"It's the next gate," David said. "Over there!"

The fivesome, plus Melody in her brother's arms, stopped at Gate 9. All of them were breathing hard, sweat dripping into their eyes. The last people were lined up, having their boarding passes checked by a uniformed Southwest Air employee before they boarded the flight.

There was no sign of Liza or Greg anywhere.

"I don't see them," Cassie whispered sadly, sagging against the wall. "They must already be on the plane."

"We're too late," Annie said.

Breezy felt tears coming to her eyes. It was all over. She had failed. Greg and Liza were eloping. The wedding was off. And there wasn't a thing she could do about it.

22

"**B**reezy?" an incredulous voice asked.

Breezy turned around.

There were her sister and Greg.

"What are you doing here?" Liza demanded.

"You're not on the plane yet?" Breezy asked, astonished that her sister was standing in front of her.

"I was in the bathroom, and — what are you doing here?" her sister repeated.

"And how did you know we were here?" Greg added.

"Please don't be mad at me," Breezy begged. "I found the plane information on your nightstand, Liza. And I thought, I thought . . ."

Now that Breezy was actually here, actually standing in front of Liza and Greg, she felt pretty stupid. Maybe it had been a dumb idea. Maybe she had no right to try and interfere with their plans. She just didn't feel sure about anything anymore.

Greg gave Breezy a jaded look. "You thought what?"

Breezy looked down at the carpet. "I'm sorry. I . . . we . . . we shouldn't be here. It's just that I saw the letter you started to Mom, Liza, and I . . ."

Breezy couldn't finish her sentence. What had seemed so clear to her before now seemed murky. Maybe her brilliant idea wasn't so brilliant after all.

"Ahem," Cassie said, clearing her throat.

Breezy looked up. And there stood Cassie, in Breezy's grandmother's wedding veil, with David standing next to her in Breezy's grandfather's top hat. With Cassie in her cutoffs and summer blouse and David in his baggy jeans and T-shirt, they looked truly ridiculous.

And incredibly sweet.

Liza put her hand over her mouth. "I don't believe it!" she exclaimed. "That's Grandma Kay's wedding veil! And Grandpa Paul's wedding top hat, right?"

Breezy nodded. She'd packed those items from the clubhouse into her backpack and had some crazy idea that having Liza and Greg see them would make them change their minds. Evidently Cassie and David had gotten the stuff out of her backpack.

The old-fashioned top hat was way too big on David, and it kept falling down onto his face.

Cassie's huge white veil kept getting caught in her mouth. Still, they both stood there as the people streaming by in the terminal gawked and laughed.

"Excuse me, but if you're on this flight to Reno, we're about to close the doors to the plane. It's now or never," the flight attendant told Liza and Greg.

"Yes," Liza said. "Just a minute . . ."

Cassie took Liza's hand. "Liza, you deserve to have the wedding you've always dreamed of."

Liza smiled fondly at the girl in the old-fashioned veil. "But it's not just my wedding," she explained gently. "It's Greg's, too." She linked her arm through Greg's. "Being married to Greg is more important to me than what kind of wedding we have."

Greg's eyes met Liza's. Breezy couldn't tell for sure, but she thought she saw some regret there. Maybe.

Liza reached out and tenderly touched Breezy's hair. "You are the sweetest little sister in the entire universe." Her eyes scanned the group. "All of you. To know that you care about us this much, but . . ." She looked over at Greg, who now was looking at the floor. "I guess it's too late now."

For a moment, Greg and Liza just stared at each other. Breezy held her breath. Maybe there was still a chance.

But then Greg picked up their small suitcases

and turned toward the entry gate. With one last smile at her little sister, Liza turned around to join her husband-to-be.

So this is how it's going to end? Breezy wondered. *Liza and Greg just get on the plane and go to Reno and elope, even if they end up regretting it for the rest of their lives?*

Greg and Liza were almost through the entry gate now, almost out of sight.

"Wait!" Breezy yelled.

Greg and Liza turned back to her.

Breezy gulped hard. Everyone stared at her, waiting. And then Breezy moved closer to the entry gate and her friends followed her. She held her head high and began to recite a certain poem she had memorized long, long ago.

I used to dream I'd be a baseball star.
Or a race car driver with the fastest car.
But now I know that if those dreams come true
They wouldn't mean a thing without you.

I know I'll love you till the end of time.
And one day I will ask you to be mine
We'll have the biggest wedding ever seen.
And they'll recall we fell in love when we were just thirteen.

Tears filled Liza's eyes. "That's the poem Greg wrote to me when we were kids. How did you — "

"Don't you remember, Liza?" Breezy asked. "I used to make you tell it to me all the time. I thought it was the most romantic thing in the world. I guess I just memorized it."

"I'm sorry, but if you don't board now, we're taking off for Reno without you," the flight attendant told Greg and Liza, her voice sharp. "We're on a schedule here."

Greg looked at Liza lovingly. His eyes were tearing up, too. "I was quite a poet, huh?"

"The best," Liza told him. "And you still are the best."

He smiled at her. "What the heck, Liza. I think eloping is highly overrated."

Liza's eyes grew huge. "You mean — ?"

"I mean I promised you a big wedding back when I was thirteen years old. Maybe I was smarter then than I like to think I am now."

Greg turned to the flight attendant. "Give our seats away. We're not getting on the plane."

Annie grinned at her big brother and punched him playfully in the bicep. "Sometimes you're okay, you know that?"

Liza threw her arms around Greg and hugged him hard. He whirled her off the ground in a circle. Some people passing by smiled at them fondly.

"They're in love," Cassie explained to the passers-by. "They're getting married."

"I want to get married, too!" Melody insisted.

"Greg, thank you!" Liza said, staring into his eyes with love.

"I was being kind of a brat about the whole thing," Greg admitted.

"He learned that from me," Annie put in proudly, and everyone laughed.

Liza took both of Greg's hands in hers. "Listen, I've been thinking. I can compromise, too, you know. How about if instead of going to Hawaii on our honeymoon, we go camping in Maine like you wanted. Then we can use the money your parents gave us for grad school, and — "

"You mean it?" Greg asked, his eyes lighting up.

"I mean it," Liza said.

"Yahoo!" Greg cried. "You're the greatest, you know that?" He picked Liza up again, kissed her softly, then forgot to stop kissing her.

Through the wedding veil that she still wore, Cassie's eyes were glued to the kiss. David was looking everyplace in the airport *except* at the kiss.

"Oooooh," Melody said, then put her hand over her mouth and giggled.

"Oh, man, this is too mushy for me," Ben grumbled, red-faced.

"Ditto," Annie agreed.

"Uh, Liza?" Breezy asked. "Earth to Liza?"

Liza finally remembered where she was and broke out of Greg's embrace. "I am so happy," she told them all. "And I have the greatest little sister."

Still holding Liza's hand, Greg turned to Breezy. "Hey, I'm really glad you're going to be my little sister, too, kiddo."

"Yeah, yeah, you can't even handle me," Annie teased.

Liza smiled at Annie. "I'm glad you're going to be my little sister, too."

Cassie carefully took off her veil. She was happy that everything was working out, but she couldn't help but feel a little left out. Now Breezy and Annie would be more than best friends. They'd be sisters, almost.

As if Melody could read Cassie's mind, she put her little hand in Cassie's and piped up, "I'm Cassie's little sister, you know." Of course, that wasn't true, but it made Cassie feel a little better.

Greg kissed Liza again, sweetly this time. Cassie sighed at the romance of it all. Was there anything better in the whole wide world than true love? She didn't think so.

"I don't see why grown-ups have to kiss all the time," Melody said, making a face.

"Me either," Ben agreed.

David took off the oversize top hat and fiddled with the brim. "I guess kissing can be okay. If you kiss the right person, that is."

Then, to Cassie's great shock, David Silver looked straight at her.

23

"It really happened, Breezy, didn't it?" Cassie asked her friend for the hundredth time. "David Silver really looked at me and —"

"I'll give you the same answer I've given you every other time you asked me," Breezy said, peeking outside the tent that had been erected at the far end of the grove at the Botanical Gardens. This tent was for Liza, the moms, Liza's bridesmaids, and her flower girl. There was another, similar tent for Greg and the guys who were in the wedding party. "David Silver really did talk about kissing and then he really did look at you."

"It really did happen." Cassie marveled at her own good fortune.

Breezy looked at the rows and rows of wedding guests, seated in white folding chairs that had been set up on either side of a long white satin carpet. "There are a zillion people out there."

"It was really sweet of Liza to ask me to be a

junior bridesmaid, too, at the last minute," Cassie said. "And it was so nice of your aunt Faith to make my dress. Do you think David will like this dress on me? Do you see him out there?" Cassie joined Breezy in peeking through a hole in the tent.

"Cassie, in just ten minutes we will all be walking down that long white satin carpet strewn with those really beautiful rose petals, and Liza and Greg will get married," Breezy said. "There's only one little problem, which seems to have escaped your David Silver-saturated mind. Annie isn't here!"

"I know that," Cassie said with indignance. "Do you see David anywhere?"

"Cassie! Enough with David. Annie should have been here forty-five minutes ago!" Breezy peered out again, her eyes searching for Annie.

"Well, she still isn't speaking to me," Cassie reminded Breezy, "so she certainly didn't tell me where she is."

"Breezy, where's Annie?" Breezy's mother asked, dodging past Liza's bridesmaids and hurrying over to the girls. She looked lovely in a floor-length pink satin suit.

"I have no idea," Breezy said. "Did you ask her mom?"

"She said she thought Annie said she was coming over with you," Mrs. Zeeman said, fanning her face with her hand, "but Paula is so stressed out right now that frankly I don't think she knows what day of the week it is."

"Well, she didn't come with me," Breezy said. "But I can't believe that after everything everyone has been through, Annie won't show up for the wedding!"

Mrs. Zeeman shook her head ruefully. Her mother had heard the whole story about how Liza and Greg had almost eloped, and how her younger daughter and her friends had been the ones to stop them. Of course, she still didn't know a thing about Annie and Cassie's big fight. Or that Breezy had promised Mrs. Anders over the phone that she would have the signed contract back to her the following morning, even if she had to bring it over on her bike. Breezy figured her mother had enough on her mind.

"I'd get worried, but if I did, who would calm Paula down?" Breezy's mom asked, nervously straightening the corsage of pink and white roses on her lapel. She caught Paula's eye from the other side of the tent, and gave her a reassuring wave.

"I am sure Annie wouldn't let us all down," Breezy insisted.

"I'm not," Cassie said under her breath, peeking out of the tent again.

"Oops, Paula is motioning for me," Mrs. Zeeman said. "Time to go handle the next crisis." She turned to Breezy. "Promise me you won't get married for a long, long time," she added, then hurried off.

"Maybe Annie really *would* mess up the wedding on purpose," Cassie mused to Breezy. "After all, once I thought I knew what kind of a person she was, but I was completely wrong."

"Cassie, Annie swears she didn't take your stuff out of the hope chest. Can't you believe her? Are you going to be mad at her for the rest of your life?"

"Aren't you?" Cassie asked. "How can I ever trust her again? How can you?"

"But there has to be some reasonable explanation for why your stuff was missing, and if the two of you would only — "

"Hey, Breezer," Annie said, rushing into the tent. "Sorry I'm late." She barely nodded at Cassie.

"Where have you been?" Breezy demanded. "You're so late! And the moms have been crazed!"

Annie was wearing her junior bridesmaid's dress, but her hair was still pinned up sloppily under her Cubs baseball cap.

"I was at the park playing one-on-one with this high-school freshman guy who thinks he's so hot," Annie explained. "At first he beat me bad. So of course I had to challenge him to a rematch. And then I dusted him."

Cassie couldn't help herself, even if it was Annie she was talking to. "In that dress?"

"No," Annie replied, "not in this dress. You think I want to let anyone see me in this dress unless I have to? The thing is, I didn't realize it was so late. I had my dress with me, because I was going to come to your house, Breezer, and get ready. So when I saw how late it was, I asked this guy's older brother to drop me off, and here I am."

"You are so inconsiderate," Cassie told her.

Annie gave her a cool look and turned back to Breezy. "So listen, I was thinking, did you call Mrs. Anders and tell her we can't work Crystal's wedding yet?"

"No," she admitted. "I keep putting it off. I told her I'd bring over the contract tomorrow."

"Well, how about if you and I work on Crystal's wedding? We can be AB Weddings."

"Oh, that's really nice," Cassie said, hurt. "You're ruining everything!"

"I'm not ruining anything," Annie maintained, "because I didn't do anything wrong in the first place!"

"Right," Cassie sniffed. "I believe you."

"You guys, can't we just — " Breezy began.

"Annie, thank heavens!" her mother cried, rushing over to her. "Where have you been?"

Annie opened her mouth to reply.

"Never mind," Mrs. McGee said, holding her hand up to Annie, "I don't even want to know.

You have your baseball cap on!" She looked aghast at Annie's head.

"Oh, yeah, I forgot," Annie said easily. She took off her baseball cap and shook her curls free.

"But you're supposed to have your hair completely off your face, and wear the satin headband that matches Breezy's and Cassie's satin headbands!" her mother exclaimed. "We planned this!"

Annie looked at Breezy and Cassie's hair. Sure enough, they were both wearing the stupid satin headbands.

"Sorry, Mom," Annie said. "I guess I forgot that, too."

Mrs. McGee fanned herself with her hand. "I may never make it through this day. Well, at least you're here." She hurried off.

Annie peered around Breezy. "Is my mom far enough away that she can't see me?"

"Yes, she's all the way over there with Liza and my mom," Breezy said.

"Good," Annie said. "Because if she saw this, she would probably faint." Annie lifted the bottom of her junior bridesmaid's dress, and instead of the dyed-to-match satin shoes she should have been wearing, there were her sneakers, which still had a faint stain on them from Scotty the Barfer.

"I kind of forgot my shoes, too."

"You would," Cassie said with disgust.

"Oh, excuse me for not being as perfect as you are," Annie jeered at Cassie. "Give me a break, it's just a pair of shoes."

"It isn't just — "

"Girls, girls, we're starting!" Mrs. McGee said, her voice rising over everyone else's. "Everyone, get in line and we'll meet the guys at the rear of the carpet. Bridesmaids, remember to take the arm of your groomsman. Where's Charlene?"

"I'm right here, Aunt Paula," a little girl in white frills carrying a basket of rose petals said.

"Okay, flower girl," Mrs. McGee said, hugging the little girl. "You get in line, too. Where's Liza? She was just here — "

"I'm right here, Paula," Liza said serenely.

Breezy looked at her sister. She had chosen a breathtakingly beautiful white wedding gown. The scoop neckline showed off a single strand of her grandmother's pearls. The full skirt was beaded with tiny seed pearls that glistened against the graceful folds of the gown. And on her head was Grandma Kay's wedding veil.

"Liza, you look so beautiful," Breezy told her sister.

Liza kissed Breezy on the cheek. "You're the best sister anyone ever had, Breezy."

Breezy felt like crying, but she forced the tears away. Instead, she carefully hugged her sister and wished her luck.

Mrs. Zeeman tucked her hand under Liza's

arm. "Liza, remember, sweetheart, you and I will wait here in the tent. Then your dad will meet us at the back of the carpet, and he and I will walk you down the aisle."

Liza smiled at her mother. "Mom, Paula, thank you for everything. I mean that with all my heart. I love you both."

As Liza and the moms hugged and tried to keep from crying, Cassie sighed with happiness. Everything for the wedding was just so perfect. An elegant all-white horse-drawn carriage had brought Liza to the Botanical Gardens. The driver was waiting to whisk Liza and Greg away for a short, romantic ride after the ceremony and before the party at the country club. Liza's wedding gown was amazing. It was all just so . . . perfect.

Someday that will be me, Cassie thought, misty-eyed. *Someday*.

"I couldn't ask for a more wonderful daughter-in-law," Mrs. McGee said, sniffling. She wiped carefully under her eyes. "Did my mascara run?"

"You're perfect, Mom," Annie assured her.

"We all love you, Liza," her mother said. She sniffed back her own tears. "Okay, everyone, let's get this show on the road."

"Today a young man and a young woman stand before us, their loving families, their friends, and their community, to pledge their love and commitment to each other."

Breezy stood to the side with Annie and Cassie, matching bouquets of white roses in their hands, and watched as Liza smiled tenderly up at Greg. Then she looked over at her parents, who were now seated in the front row with Greg's parents. Both the moms were crying, and Breezy was pretty sure she saw tears in her dad's eyes, too.

"It's so beautiful," Cassie whispered to her.

Breezy nodded, feeling herself getting choked up, too. All of Liza's bridesmaids, in their matching pink chiffon floor-length gowns, were standing just to the side of the junior bridesmaids, teary-eyed.

It seemed as if everyone was crying with happiness. Even Annie had a tear or two, which she wiped away quickly lest anyone see.

"Do you, Liza Anne Zeeman, take this man, Gregory Michael McGee, to be your lawfully wedded husband, in sickness and in health, in good times and in bad, till death do you part?" asked the judge.

"I do," Liza said in a clear voice.

"And do you, Gregory Michael McGee, take this woman, Liza Anne Zeeman, to be your lawfully wedded wife, in sickness and in health, in good times and in bad, till death do you part?"

"I *definitely* do," Greg said, and everyone laughed.

"If any person here has reason why these two young people should not be joined together, let them speak now, or forever hold their peace."

No one spoke. The only sound was the tiniest breeze ruffling through the gardens, and the calls of the birds that flew overhead. At that moment, Greg and Liza both turned their heads away from the judge and looked at Breezy, Cassie, and Annie.

"Thank you," Liza mouthed at them.

Greg nodded in agreement and gave them the thumbs-up sign.

"We did it, you guys," Breezy whispered, her eyes tearing up again. "We helped make this happen."

"I love happy endings," Cassie whispered back.

Annie scuffed the toe of one hidden gym shoe into the grass underfoot. "Too bad some things don't work out that way," she added, her voice low.

Breezy knew she meant the three of them. Once it had seemed impossible that the three of them would ever, ever break up their friendship, and it had seemed very possible that Liza and Greg would never, ever get married — at least, not in a big wedding like this.

But look what had happened. Life was just so strange and unpredictable sometimes. Breezy wanted to believe that if she just worked hard enough, she could always make things work out the way she wanted them to. But now she could see that some things were just out of a person's control. Even hers. It was an awfully scary thought.

" . . . by the power vested in me by the state of Indiana, I now pronounce you husband and wife. You may kiss the bride."

Greg took Liza into his arms and kissed her.

Some people cheered, others applauded, and still others dabbed at the happy tears in their eyes as the string quartet began to play "I Will Always Love You." Then the newly married Greg and Liza, who both seemed to shine from within, walked hand in hand toward their friends and family, and into their new life.

24

"What a wedding, huh?" David asked Cassie over the sound of the oldies band that was playing on a small stage that overlooked the dance floor. Many couples were dancing, and others were eating the sumptuous food from the buffet, or laughing and talking with their friends.

"It's the best wedding I've ever been to," Cassie agreed. She saw Breezy talking to some of her cousins and Annie standing near the buffet with Ben, trying to balance a fork on the end of her finger.

David stuck his hands into the pocket of his suit pants. "So . . . you look really nice in that dress."

Cassie's heart swelled with happiness. Maybe he really *did* like her! Maybe he really *had* been looking at her at the airport when he said —

And then a terrible, awful, horrible thought flew into Cassie's head. Suddenly she knew. It all made sense. She knew why David Silver was being so nice to her.

It had to be because Annie had shown David the photo of him that Cassie had put in the hope chest, and probably the short story, too. Maybe the two of them had laughed at her. And now David was only being nice to her because he felt sorry for her.

It had to be. It was the only thing that made sense. She would never forgive Annie for this. Never, never, never. And she would never forgive David, either.

Cassie's hands formed tight fists at her sides. "Look, I know what happened," she blurted out.

"What?" David asked, looking confused.

"I know what Annie did, okay?"

"What are you talking about?" David asked.

"I know you know, so don't pretend you don't," Cassie insisted.

"Know w*hat*?"

"I'm sorry I ever even liked you, David Silver!" Cassie cried. "So just forget the whole thing!" Cassie ran, tears streaming down her face, to the only place she could think of where she could face her humiliation in private — the country club's ladies' room.

She ran inside and leaned against the wall, crying bitter tears, her arms wrapped around her waist. How could Annie do this to her?

How?

"Cassie?"

Cassie looked up. It was Melody.

"Are you okay?" the little girl asked. "I saw you run in here and you looked sad."

"I am sad, kind of," Cassie admitted, fisting the tears off her cheeks.

"That makes me sad, too," Melody said. "Did you fall and get a boo-boo?"

"No," Cassie said, sniffing back her tears. "Someone just . . . someone who I thought was one of my two best friends in the whole world did something really, really mean to me."

"What?" Melody asked. She looked as if she, too, was going to cry at any moment.

"It doesn't matter anymore," Cassie said, feeling defeated.

"Oh," Melody said. She leaned against the wall with Cassie. "Hey, know what?"

"What?"

"I have a purse," Melody said. "Just like a big girl." She held her pink patent leather purse out for Cassie to see.

"Very pretty," Cassie told her. She pushed herself off the wall. "Well, I guess I'd better wash my face, huh?"

"And put on more lipstick," Melody said seriously. "That's what you're supposed to do. I have candy lipstick in my purse. Wanna see?"

Cassie felt so miserable that she really didn't want to see Melody's candy lipstick, but she loved the little girl too much to tell her that. So she peered into Melody's purse as the little girl opened it.

"See?" Melody said. "It's pink, and — "

The look on Cassie's face made Melody stop. Cassie was still staring into her purse.

"I don't believe it," Cassie breathed.

"What?" Melody asked. She looked inside her purse, too.

Sure enough, there was her candy lipstick. And there was the little photo of her big brother. And the folded-up piece of notebook paper she had taken from the —

Oops.

Now Melody remembered. She really wasn't supposed to open that secret hope chest in the clubhouse. She was only an honorary little sister. She couldn't really be in the club until she was a teenager, which was a long, long time away.

Melody looked up at Cassie. "Are you mad at me?"

Cassie reached into Melody's purse and took out David's photo, as well as the very romantic short story she had written about Prince David and Princess Cassie.

"Melody, where did you get these?"

The little girl's lower lip trembled and she was on the brink of tears. "Did I do bad?"

Cassie shook her head as if to clear out the confusion, but she still didn't understand. "Mel, how did you get these?"

Melody hung her head. "When you took me to see the clubhouse and you went to the bathroom, I found these in the secret hope chest," she admitted.

"But the hope chest was locked. I locked it. I'm sure I locked it."

Melody shook her head no. "I just opened it right up. I know you told me not to touch anything. I guess you're not . . . " Melody struggled to remember the new word Cassie had taught her. And then she remembered. "I guess you're not honored anymore."

For a moment, Cassie couldn't move, couldn't speak, as the truth about everything hit her. Annie hadn't stolen her things from the hope chest. She really had been innocent. And David Silver had just been nice to her because, well, because he wanted to be.

"Cassie?" Melody looked up at her idol, tears streaming down her cheeks.

Cassie knelt down and hugged the little girl hard. "You shouldn't have opened up the hope chest and taken anything out without asking, but I'm not mad at you."

"Will you still be my friend?" Melody asked in a small voice.

"Of course I'll be your friend," Cassie said, hugging her again. Quickly, Cassie splashed some cold water on her face and wiped it clean.

She looked at her reflection in the mirror.

"Cassie Pearson, you have done the dumbest thing in the entire history of dumb things."

"You forgot more lipstick," Melody reminded her solemnly.

"I don't need lipstick," Cassie said. "Come on, let's go."

Cassie took Melody's hand and led her back to the party. After making Cassie reassure her one more time that she wasn't mad, the little girl ran off to see her mother.

Cassie took a deep breath and walked over to Annie.

Annie was leaning against one of the ballroom pillars, eating a plateful of food.

"Can I talk to you?" Cassie asked her.

"Why?" Annie asked her sullenly. "What am I supposed to have done wrong now?"

"Nothing," Cassie said. Nervously she pressed her lips together. "Annie, I was wrong."

Annie stopped eating and stared at her.

"I was just in the ladies' room with Melody, and . . . she had this in her purse." Cassie showed Annie the photo of David and her short story.

"But how?" Annie asked incredulously.

Quickly Cassie explained what had happened, how she had taken Melody to the clubhouse as a special treat, how the little girl had taken those things from the hope chest while Cassie was in the bathroom.

"I was so sure I had locked the hope chest,"

Cassie continued, "but I guess somehow I didn't."

"It was really, really awful having you accuse me like that, Cassie," Annie said. "It really hurt."

"I know," Cassie said. "I'm so sorry. I don't know what else to say."

Annie faced her. "How come you were so willing to believe that I'm this awful person?"

"I just couldn't think of any other explanation that made sense and I — "

"Hey, are you two actually speaking to each other?" Breezy asked hopefully, running over to them.

"I was apologizing to Annie," Cassie said. She repeated the whole story for Breezy.

"But this is fantastic!" Breezy cried happily. "You were both innocent all along!"

"Not me," Cassie said, feeling miserable. "I'm the one who didn't lock the hope chest carefully enough. And then I blamed it on one of my two best friends in the whole world."

Annie folded her arms. "You know what really gets me, Cassie? That it was just so easy for you to believe that I was the kind of person who would do something like that to you."

Cassie struggled to hold back her tears. "I know. I guess . . . well . . . I always feel like you and Breezy are best friends — I mean, now you two are even related to each other! And the clubhouse really belongs to the two of you, and I'm just this . . . this third wheel that you let tag along."

"But that is totally not true," Breezy said. "It doesn't feel right unless it's the three of us. Tell her, Annie!"

Annie looked at Cassie. "I always think that you two don't need me," she admitted.

"But how could you ever think that?" Cassie exclaimed.

"Because you're just so nice, Cassie. You're way nicer than I am. Everyone knows what a brat I can be. I mean, who wouldn't want to have you as a best friend?"

"I can't believe this!" Cassie said, laughing with relief. "I was so sure you guys didn't need me at all."

"Cassie Pearson, you just happen to be about the nicest girl I know," Annie said. "My own mother keeps hoping some of it will rub off on me."

"But you're so funny and brave and — "

"Bratty," Annie said. "I really am kind of selfish sometimes. But you — "

"Hey, you guys, please don't start arguing over which one of you is nicer!" Breezy said, laughing.

"She's right," Annie said. "Okay, I'm nicer."

They all cracked up.

"Breezer, why don't you call Mrs. Anders tonight and tell her that ABC Weddings is at her service!" Annie suggested.

"It isn't too late, is it?" Cassie asked.

"I'll tell her we'll work night and day for the next two weeks," Breezy promised happily.

From out of the corner of her eye, Cassie saw David Silver standing by himself, looking over at her. Shyly, she looked away. *How could I have said what I said to him?* she asked herself. *How am I ever going to explain?*

"Hey, let's go raid the dessert table," Annie suggested.

"I want one slice of every dessert on the table," Breezy said. "You coming, Cassie?"

"You guys go," Cassie said. "There's something I have to do first. I'll come find you."

With her knees shaking and her heart in her mouth, Cassie walked over to David Silver. "Hi."

"Hi." He didn't look at her.

"So, I guess you think I acted pretty weird before," Cassie said, leaning against a large white column.

"You could say that."

"I know," Cassie said. "I *did* act weird. The thing is, I thought something was true that turned out not to be true."

He finally turned to look at her, but he didn't say a word.

"So, well . . . I just wanted to apologize," Cassie said.

"Okay."

"So, see you."

"See you."

Cassie walked dejectedly back toward her friends. She had ruined everything with David Silver by acting so stupid. There was no way he would ever like her again after what she did. There was no way she could explain. And there was nothing she could do about it now.

I am not going to mope about it, she told herself. *I'm not going to let how I feel about David Silver wreck how happy I am about making up with Annie.*

"Okay, you guys," Cassie said when she found Breezy and Annie at the dessert table. "Just this once, I'm going to eat sugar *and* chocolate." She picked up a dessert plate and a small fork.

"Wow!" Annie exclaimed. "The next thing you know we'll get you to eat junk food with us."

"I wouldn't go that far," Cassie said as she slipped a slice of chocolate cheesecake onto her plate.

"Let's find a table," Annie said, looking around for some empty seats. "Over there, near the band."

Breezy stopped her. "You guys, wait, before we eat dessert, there's something I want to say."

"So say it," Annie said. "My ice-cream pie is melting."

"We have to promise that we're not going to fight anymore, and that we'll always trust each other."

196

"We promised stuff before," Annie reminded her. "It didn't help."

For a moment, all three of them were silent. They all knew it was true.

"Do you think any girls who are best friends when they're thirteen actually stay best friends when they're adults?" Cassie asked.

"We can," Breezy insisted. "I know we can. We just have to want to badly enough."

"I want to," Annie said.

"Me too," Cassie agreed. "Our friendship has to be more important to us than our fights, is what you're saying."

Breezy nodded. "We're three different people. We don't have to all act the same or think the same."

"Or dress the same, like we did for that one week when we were in the second grade," Annie recalled, making a face. "Boy, I *hated* the clothes you made me wear!"

Cassie looked at Annie. "I promise that our friendship will always be bigger than our differences."

"I promise, too," Annie agreed. "Hey, we're even in business again. I hope we all make a mint on Crystal's wedding!"

"Just think how much fun it will be," Cassie said, "working on a wedding for a famous model. Do you think any of the supermodels will be at the wedding?"

"Mrs. Anders says Crystal works with all of them," Breezy said, "so maybe."

"I'll make sure I get photos of all of them for you," Annie offered.

Cassie shook her head. "I can't believe how dumb I was, Annie, believing that you would do something horrible to me and then lie about it."

"Yeah, you were a dope," Annie said, but she had a big grin on her face as she said it.

"Best friends forever," Cassie said. From under the neckline of her bridesmaid's dress, she pulled out the chain that held her key to the hope chest.

Wordlessly, Annie and Breezy pulled theirs out, too.

"None of us ever stopped wearing them," Breezy marveled.

"This is so great," Cassie said, her eyes shining. "Even if I did ruin everything with David Silver — you guys are never going to believe what I did — this is more important because — "

Cassie was interrupted by a tap on her shoulder.

She turned around.

It was David Silver.

"Would you like to dance?" he asked Cassie.

"I'd love to dance," Cassie replied. She handed her dessert plate to Breezy.

As her two grinning best friends looked on, a blissfully happy Cassie stepped into David Silver's arms, and finally they danced.

25

"**W**ant a bite?" Annie asked as she offered the corn dog Mrs. Anders had just bought her to Breezy.

"No thanks," Breezy answered. She looked down at her lap, where the fallout from a big bag of popcorn lay in little kernels on her jeans. They had been waiting for Crystal's plane to arrive for almost two hours, and she had eaten her way through two giant pretzels, one candy bar, and one huge bag of popcorn.

It was two days after Liza and Greg's wedding, and the girls were doing their very first assignment for Mrs. Anders. She had asked them to come with her to the airport to meet Crystal so that they could help with Crystal's most cherished possession, Tiffany, a prizewinning toy poodle, who was arriving on the same plane. Breezy had assured Mrs. Anders that they already had a lot of experience with dogs.

"Well, this is intensely boring," Annie said as

199

she polished off her second corn dog. She watched yet another airplane taxi past the window on the runway outside the terminal. "I'm sitting in the Indianapolis airport, waiting for a dog."

"But you're getting paid to do it," Cassie reminded her. She looked across the way at Mrs. Anders, who was busy speaking with an employee from the airline and waving her hands around a lot. "From the looks of Mrs. Anders over there, I'd say she isn't getting good news about Crystal's flight."

Mrs. Anders walked briskly back over to the girls, her many silver and gold bangle bracelets jingling on her arms as she walked. "The utter incompetence! My Crystal's flight was held up in New York because of fog in Cleveland or something. None of it made any sense to me. Now they're telling me the flight will arrive any minute. Of course, they also told me that thirty minutes ago. Something about headwinds or tailwinds or . . ." She threw her hands into the air as if to say, "I give up."

"Why don't you just sit down and we can check on the flight from now on," Breezy offered. She felt guilty that they were getting paid for just sitting there.

Mrs. Anders took a seat next to Breezy, but one high-heeled shoe tapped nervously against the other. "Waiting like this just makes me insane." She turned to Breezy. "Have you heard from your sister and Greg? How's their honeymoon going?"

"They called yesterday," Breezy reported. "They were in a diner in . . . what was the name of that town, Annie?"

"Machias, Maine," Annie reported.

"Right," Breezy said, nodding. "They're driving up to the Saint Croix River to go smallmouth bass fishing."

"Yuck," Cassie said, wrinkling her nose. "And to think they gave up Hawaii for that."

"I'm with you," Mrs. Anders said.

"My dumb married brother managed to get poison ivy already," Annie said.

"Poison ivy on a honeymoon — not very romantic," Cassie said. "I don't think you can even kiss someone with poison ivy, can you?"

Annie wriggled her eyebrows at Cassie. "I bet you'd still kiss David Silver if he had poison ivy."

"Attention, attention, National Airlines Flight Eighty-two from New York's LaGuardia Airport has just landed and will be arriving at Gate Seventeen. I repeat, National Airlines Flight Eighty-two will be arriving at Gate Seventeen. Thank you."

"Finally!" Mrs. Anders exclaimed, jumping up from her seat. The four of them walked over to wait by the gate.

"Will she be carrying her dog with her, Mrs. Anders?" Breezy asked.

"No," Mrs. Anders said. "The airline is bar-

baric. They forced poor little Tiffany to ride underneath the plane with the luggage. It isn't human!"

"Neither is a dog," Annie said under her breath.

Cassie giggled but nudged Annie to keep her mouth shut.

"I can't wait to see my Crystal," Mrs. Anders said. "We're as close as sisters, she and I. We always have been. When my Crystal was born I told the doctor she was so perfect I wished she had been twins." She turned to a uniformed employee of the airline who was writing something into a chart. "Where is the plane? I thought it landed."

"It will be a few minutes before the plane can taxi into the gate, ma'am," the employee said. "There are a number of planes waiting to taxi in right now."

"Girls, I'm going to run and freshen up quickly," Mrs. Anders said. "I want to look perfect for my Crystal. Don't move a muscle." She hurried to the ladies' room, which was opposite the next gate.

"What's up with this 'my Crystal' thing?" Annie asked when Mrs. Anders was out of earshot. "It sounds like she's talking about her glassware."

"She's just excited that she's going to see her daughter," Breezy explained, leaning against the wall.

202

"And she's proud of her," Cassie added. "I don't blame her. Can you imagine if your daughter became a supermodel? What mother wouldn't be proud of that?"

"Mine," Annie said, fiddling with the brim of her Cubs baseball cap. "For one thing, my mom is a feminist, so she'd be more proud if I became, like, President of the United States or something."

"You're more likely to become first base-*person* for the Cubs," Breezy said, laughing.

"I wish." Annie looked at her Mickey Mouse watch. "Speaking of the Cubs, I've got baseball practice at six, and it's already four-thirty. So unless Mrs. Anders wants to pinch-hit for me, I hope we can move this along."

"There's the plane." Cassie pointed out the window.

"She's here!" Mrs. Anders cried, hurrying back over to the girls. She clasped her perfectly manicured hands together. "My Crystal!"

Behind Mrs. Anders's back, Annie silently mimicked her. Cassie bit her lip to keep from laughing out loud.

The first few well-dressed people came out of the gate.

"Where's my Crystal?" Mrs. Anders asked, craning her neck. "She always flies first class!"

"There she is," Breezy said, pointing.

"Wow," Cassie breathed. "That's Crystal?"

Breezy was stunned. It was easy to tell that the young woman walking toward her was an older version of the teenage girl who had baby-sat for her. She really hadn't changed that much. But the teenage Crystal had been a casual, energetic, healthy kind of girl who lived in jeans, T-shirts, and sneakers. She had always had a smile on her face. The rake-thin Crystal who was approaching now wore a long black tunic over slender black pants with sky-high black platform shoes. Oversized black sunglasses covered her eyes. And the look on her face was as dark as her outfit.

"Wow," Cassie said again, gape-mouthed. "I saw that outfit she's wearing on a fashion show on VH1. It's by some famous French designer."

"She's changed from when she used to be my baby-sitter," Breezy said.

"She was just a child then," Mrs. Anders said. "Crystal!" she called, waving her hand in the air. "Crystal, darling!" She ran to her daughter and hugged her hard. Crystal looked as if she was suffering through the embrace.

"Hello, Mother," Crystal said coolly when her mother finally released her. She leaned over and kissed her mother on one cheek and then the other. "Now, isn't that a more civilized way for us to greet each other?"

"Very European," Mrs. Anders said, nodding in agreement. She turned to the girls, who stood just behind her. "Crystal dear, do you recognize any of these darling young ladies?"

Behind her dark sunglasses, Crystal's eyes scanned the girls. "Am I supposed to?"

"Remember I told you I hired three darling girls to help Perfect Weddings do your wedding? You used to baby-sit for one of them?"

"Baby-sitting," Crystal said. "Who could believe that I was ever a baby-sitter?"

"I could," Breezy said with excitement. "It's me, Breezy Zeeman. You were my favorite baby-sitter of all time, Crystal."

Crystal took off her sunglasses. "Breezy?" she asked, her voice a little distant.

Breezy smiled. "It's me! Wow, it is so great to see you. I can't believe we're working on your wedding, and — "

"Breezy is rather a silly name, don't you think?" Crystal sniffed. "I like the name Brianna better." She put her sunglasses back on. "That flight took forever, Mother. I have a splitting headache."

"My poor baby," Mrs. Anders sympathized. "Why don't I take you out to the van and — "

"You're driving a *van*?" Crystal asked, as if the word "van" really meant "garbage."

"I like it, actually," Mrs. Anders said. "Anyway, why don't I take you to the van and the girls can get your luggage and Tiffany and come meet us."

She turned to Breezy. "Can the three of you handle that?"

"Certainly," Breezy assured her. "We'll need the luggage claims and the claim for Tiffany, please." She still felt stung from how nasty Crystal had been to her. It hardly seemed possible that Crystal was the same girl who used to be such a terrific baby-sitter.

Crystal handed the claim tickets to Breezy. "Be very, very careful with Tiffany," she warned. "I'm sure she's utterly traumatized by all this."

Mrs. Anders handed Breezy a handful of dollar bills. "Once you find everything, just ask one of the skycaps to load it up for you. Be sure you tip them for their service. I'll meet all of you just outside in front with the van."

"Fine," Breezy said.

"Mother, are you sure these three little girls can handle this?" Crystal asked dubiously.

"We happen to be a professional business," Annie said. "ABC Weddings. By the way, my name is Annie McGee, and this is Cassie Pearson, since you didn't bother to ask."

"My Crystal has had a very trying day," Mrs. Anders said, excusing her daughter's behavior. "Breezy, I will consider this a test of whether or not you and your little friends are mature enough to handle working on my Crystal's wedding."

"We can handle it," Cassie assured her.

"Well, that's very sweet," Crystal said, "but

Tiffany only responds to me. You girls can get my luggage."

They headed toward the luggage claim area, Crystal striding ahead in her five-inch platform shoes, the others hurrying to keep up.

"Hold it," Crystal said, stopping in front of a ladies' room. She hurried inside.

She ducked inside, and Mrs. Anders and the girls were forced to wait as five minutes passed, and then ten.

"I'll go see if my Crystal is all right," Mrs. Anders finally said, heading into the ladies' room.

"Yuck," Annie said. "Her Crystal is a real pain in the butt, huh?"

"She really used to be nice, Breezy?" Cassie asked.

Breezy nodded. "She doesn't even seem like the same person."

"Well, she's a famous model now," Cassie considered. "I guess that changes a person."

"Get real," Annie said. "If she's so famous, how come we've never seen her picture in any magazines or anything?"

"Shhh, here they come," Cassie hissed.

Crystal strode over to them, her mother behind her.

"You're still here?" she asked the girls. "I thought you'd have gotten my bags by now!"

"You asked us to wait for you," Breezy reminded her.

"I didn't mean wait *here*," Crystal said, as if Breezy were beyond stupid.

"Don't blame the girls," Mrs. Anders said mildly. "I thought you meant for us to wait here for you, too."

Crystal let out a long-suffering sigh. "Fine. Just fine. Can we please go now, then?"

Crystal led the procession through the airport, down the escalator to the baggage claim area, and over to the carousel that held the luggage from the New York to Indianapolis flight. Most of the people on the flight had picked up their baggage already, but eight or ten bags were still revolving on the conveyor belt.

And seven of them were from an identical set of designer luggage, all jumbo-sized.

"Oh, no," Annie moaned, figuring out what was going on.

"That one's mine," Crystal said, pointing to one of the matching pieces on the carousel. "And that one. And that one. And that one and that one and that one and that one."

"We get the idea," Annie mumbled, reaching for one of the jumbo suitcases.

"No, dear," Mrs. Anders said, stopping her. "Ask the skycap to load them for you while I go help Crystal collect Tiffany."

Breezy politely asked a skycap to help them, and he quickly loaded all of Crystal's luggage onto a rolling cart. "Where to, young ladies?"

They looked around. Coming toward them were Mrs. Anders and Crystal. Crystal was carrying a small silver cage, which clearly held a small barking dog.

"Oh, very good," Mrs. Anders said when she saw the skycap patiently waiting with the luggage. "I'll just run and get the van and bring it to the front. If you could bring the luggage out there, sir, and load it into my van . . ."

"You got it," the friendly skycap agreed, rolling the cart toward the automatic glass doors.

"My poor baby," Crystal crooned to the dog inside the silver cage. "Do you want to meet the girls who are going to take care of you for a while? This is Brianna . . . and her two little friends." She turned to the girls. "And *this*," she added momentously, "is Tiffany."

The girls peered inside the cage. Tiffany was a tiny toy poodle. Her white fur had been cut and sculpted into puffballs, the ends of which were dyed pale pink. There was a pink ribbon behind each ear. Around her neck was a pink rhinestone dog collar. Even her toenails were painted pink.

"Gee . . ." was all Breezy could manage.

"Who did that to the dog?" Annie asked, wrinkling her nose.

"Isn't she the most precious?" Crystal cooed into the silver cage. "Crystal loves her wittle Tiffany, yes she does."

"Do you want me to carry Tiffany?" Breezy offered.

"Be very careful," Crystal warned, handing the caged Tiffany over. "She's very emotional and high-strung."

Out of her large black leather bag she pulled some bottled water and guzzled some down. "Air travel is so dehydrating."

"Can't you just get a drink at a water fountain?" Annie asked.

Crystal looked horrified. "That water is absolute poison. I wouldn't even let Tiffany drink that! She drinks only purified water, and she eats a special health mix that I have custom-made for her. I just gave her a little treat of it when I picked her up. My poor baby was starving." She put her water back in her purse. "I'll meet you three at the van." She hurried on her tottering shoes toward the doors.

Annie looked at Tiffany, who was panting in the cage. "If you ask me, this dog looks possessed. Do you think her beady little eyes roll all the way back in her head?"

"Come on," Cassie chided, "it's not the dog's fault that Crystal made her into a circus pooch. Actually, she looks kind of cute."

"Not," Annie grunted.

Tiffany began to bark at Annie. Annie barked back.

"Cut it out," Breezy said, laughing in spite of herself.

"I can't believe we're stuck with this little rat for almost two weeks," Annie said as they walked toward the door. Tiffany continued to bark.

"Hey, we handled three dogs just a few weeks ago," Cassie reminded her.

Tiffany began to make a funny mewling whine. The girls stopped and looked into the cage.

"Is she sick, do you think?" Cassie asked anxiously.

The whining grew louder. And then, suddenly, little Tiffany burped up a tiny portion of her special health mix.

"I sure am glad I don't have to clean that up," Annie said cheerfully.

"We all have to clean it up," Breezy said. "It's only fair."

"Wrong," Annie said. "Remember, you guys promised to take care of the biters and the barfers. No one ever said they had to be human." She grinned at them. "Come on. Let's get the barfer back to her mommy. I think they're just *darling* together!"

26

"Can I get you girls something cold to drink?" Mrs. Anders offered the three girls, who had just arrived at her house the next afternoon. "It's awfully hot out."

"That would be great, if it's not too much trouble," Breezy said. The bike ride over to Mrs. Anders's house had left all three girls flushed and sweaty.

"No trouble," Mrs. Anders assured them. "I'll be right back and we'll get to work. My Crystal should be down any minute. A good night's rest in her own bed did her a world of good."

"Maybe that means Crystal will be nicer today," Cassie said after Mrs. Anders left the pristine antique-filled living room.

"I hope," Annie said, leaning back against the white couch cushions.

"Me too," Breezy agreed. "Yesterday Crystal was like a completely different person — someone I didn't like very much."

"Who could be friends with a snob like her?" Annie asked.

"A snob like who?" Crystal asked, striding into the room in light blue patent leather mules with heels as high as yesterday's shoes. With the mules she wore a sky blue miniskirt and a T-shirt so tiny it looked like it belonged on a two-year-old.

"A snob like . . . this girl in our class at school," Breezy quickly fibbed.

"She used to be really nice, but she changed," Annie added mischievously.

"Uh-huh," Crystal said. It was clear she wasn't really listening. She took a seat on the white-on-white upholstered chair opposite the girls. "Where's my mother?"

"She went to get us something cold to drink," Cassie said. "Listen, if you don't mind my asking . . . I know you're a famous model and . . . well, I'd love to hear what it's like."

Crystal shrugged. "You get your picture taken a lot and make a lot of money. You get to fly to exotic places. It can be kind of boring, really."

Cassie sat forward on the couch. "Do you know Cindy Crawford and Claudia Schiffer and Kate Moss and — "

"All models know each other," Crystal said airily. "We all work together."

"I've always dreamed of being a model," Cassie confessed. "Not that I'm so perfect-looking or anything. And I guess I'd have to lose some weight — "

"You're not fat, Cassie!" Breezy exclaimed.

"I know," Cassie said, "but models have to be superthin. Right, Crystal?"

"Absolutely," Crystal said. "I used to be a little butterball, but when I first got to New York I took off twenty pounds with the help of this amazing nutritionist. She works with Tiffany, too."

Annie tried to keep a straight face. "Your nutritionist works with your dog?"

Crystal nodded. "She can read your aura and tell which foods are toxic for you."

"What's an aura?" Cassie asked.

"The invisible halo of light that surrounds each of us," Crystal explained. "My aura is gold, for example. Tiffany's is pink."

"That's a joke," Annie said. "Right?"

Crystal gave Annie a cool look. "Clearly, you are ignorant about nutrition. What do your parents feed you, white bread and bologna?"

"Uh-huh," Annie confirmed cheerfully. "And junk food. The junkier the better. My whole family likes junk food. We could live on pizza."

"Honestly, people in this little town are so provincial," Crystal sighed. She recrossed her legs. "Well, let's talk about the care of my darling little Tiffany. First of all, don't you dare ever, ever feed her any junk food. In fact, don't feed her anything that isn't on the list."

"The list?" Breezy echoed.

"My mother has it," Crystal said.

At that moment Mrs. Anders returned, carrying a tray of frosty glasses. "I hope you girls like lemonade," she said as she handed them each a glass. "Some for you, sweetheart?" she asked Crystal.

"Only if you used organic lemons and squeezed it yourself," Crystal replied loftily.

"It came from a carton, I'm afraid," Mrs. Anders said, taking a seat. "So, let's get down to business." She took a sheet of paper out of her pocket. "This is Crystal's list for the care and feeding of Tiffany."

"It has to be followed exactly," Crystal warned.

"Of course, precious," Mrs. Anders assured her daughter. Her eyes scanned the list. "Let's see . . . Tiffany is to be fed twice a day, exactly two ounces of her special health mix. You girls will purchase the ingredients fresh each day from a health food store — "

"No bulk buying," Crystal put in. "It has to be fresh."

"I thought health food stores didn't carry meat," Breezy said.

Crystal gave her an incredulous look. "Tiffany doesn't eat meat. Meat and dairy are poison."

"For a dog?" Annie asked dubiously.

"Let's move on," Mrs. Anders said. "Tiffany sometimes has a little stomach distress. You need to give her her medication with an eye dropper three times per day."

"How about if we just mix it into her food?" Annie suggested.

Crystal gave her mother a horrified look. "Mother, I don't think this is going to work out at all!"

"Calm down, dear, Annie was just asking," Mrs. Anders soothed. "Moving on, then. Tiffany must be walked three times per day. Don't allow her to get overheated. If the temperature is above eighty degrees, make sure you stop every ten minutes and allow her to drink water."

"Bottled water," Crystal added.

"Bottled water," her mother echoed. "Well, there's more, girls, but I'm sure you can read through the rest of this yourselves." She handed the list to Breezy.

"Make sure that Tiffany is perfectly groomed at all times," Crystal said. "My agent says *People* magazine may come do a spread on my wedding preparations, and I'll want Tiffany included in the photo shoot."

"*People* magazine?" Cassie asked with awe. "Are you serious? I read *People* all the time."

"Crystal, darling, you didn't tell me about

that!" Mrs. Anders cried. "That's so fabulous. Wait until I tell all my friends. They'll be green with envy!"

"When will the photographers from *People* be here?" Cassie asked eagerly.

"It isn't exactly definite yet," Crystal said. "But I need you to be prepared."

"Oh, we will be," Cassie assured her. "Do you think they might even take pictures of us?"

"I doubt it," Crystal replied.

"You know what would be so cute," Mrs. Anders said, tapping one finger against her chin in contemplation. "How about if we rounded up your girlfriends from high school who were cheerleaders with you, and *People* could run a now-and-then photo of all of you?"

"I don't know, Mother — "

"But it would be priceless!" Mrs. Anders insisted. "Those girls are just so jealous of you, you know. I run into them now and then and I tell them all about your modeling career."

Crystal smiled icily. "And to think they barely even let me on the cheerleading squad."

Mrs. Anders laughed. "That's not true, Crystal. You were the best-looking, most popular girl in your class."

"That's not how I remember it, Mother."

"Uh, excuse me, but maybe we should get Tiffany and get going," Breezy said.

"Excellent idea," Crystal agreed. "Be sure my brother hasn't poisoned my little angel over-night."

The girls all looked confused. What did Crystal's brother have to do with anything?

"Is Tiffany upstairs?" Annie asked, getting up from the couch. "I haven't heard her bark at all."

Crystal looked at her mother. "Didn't you tell them?"

"Of course I told them," Mrs. Anders replied, sipping her lemonade.

"Told us what?" Breezy asked.

"That Tiffany is staying at my son's house — the house he rents with your brother," Mrs. Anders said. "I told you."

"No, ma'am," Breezy said. "You didn't."

"I distinctly remember telling you that you'd be picking Tiffany up at Pete's, and you'd be walking all four of the dogs every day."

"Hold it, hold it, hold it," Annie said. "We're walking Tiny, Minnie, Four-Oh-Nine, *and* Tiffany? Every *day*?"

"Three times per day," Crystal said. "Tiffany absolutely must be walked three times per day."

"I know it was on my list of things to tell you," Mrs. Anders said, distressed. "I said that since Greg is on his honeymoon and Pete still has a cast on his leg, I would be paying you girls to care for all four dogs."

"I think maybe you forgot to mention this to us," Cassie said.

"Is it more than you girls can handle?" Mrs. Anders asked. "Because I can hire someone else if — "

"We can definitely handle it," Breezy interrupted. "We've taken care of the other three dogs before, so it's no problem."

"Well, that's a relief," Mrs. Anders said. She looked at her watch. "Oh, dear. Crystal, we've got to get you over to a fitting. And you girls need to hurry on over to Pete's house. Keep track of your hours, and call me if you need anything. Of course, I won't be here. I'll be with my Crystal. But you can leave a message." Much as she had with Breezy at their earlier meeting, she hustled the girls out the front door.

"I must be having a nightmare," Annie said as they unlocked their bikes. "Tell me we aren't taking care of four mutts."

"We are," Breezy said, getting on her bike.

Annie kicked up her kickstand and got on her bike, too. "Well, then, there's only one hope."

"What's that?" Cassie asked.

"That Tiny will eat Tiffany for breakfast," Annie replied. "At least Tiny isn't afraid to eat meat!"

27

"Whoa, Tiny!" Breezy called to the gigantic Saint Bernard as he tugged so hard on his leash that he practically dragged Breezy across the sidewalk. "Easy, boy!"

"He saw a squirrel," Annie pointed out as she followed close behind with Tiffany. She held Tiffany on a special pink rhinestone-studded leash that Crystal had given her. Cassie brought up the rear, with Minnie the golden retriever on one leash and Four-Oh-Nine the Chihuahua on another.

"How long have we been walking them already?" Cassie asked as Minnie stopped to sniff a fire hydrant. "I don't have a watch on."

"Fifteen minutes," Breezy replied, wiping some sweat from her forehead. "It is so hot out!"

"We're supposed to give Tiffany a break and some water," Cassie reminded them. "Bottled water."

"We don't have any bottled water," Annie said.

"And if we did, we'd be drinking it instead of giving it to the Pooch in Pink. She looks fine, and we're a sweaty mess."

Tiffany trotted along happily, as did the other dogs. So far none of them seemed to be bothered by the heat.

"After this walk we'll buy some bottled water," Breezy said. "We're getting paid to follow all of Crystal's directions."

"Like giving Tiffany that medicine with the eye dropper wasn't enough," Annie groused. "And how about mixing that awful health food? Dogs are supposed to eat meat, not soy protein."

"There's the sign for the new dog run," Cassie said, pointing with her chin, since both her hands were holding leashes.

"I guess the city had us in mind when they built it," Breezy said. "Four dogs, three dog-walkers."

"We can let the beasts run loose in the dog run and rest," Annie said as Tiffany stopped to sniff Tiny.

"I don't think Crystal is going to be too happy about Tiffany running loose," Cassie cautioned.

"Please," Annie replied. "The dog can have a new experience — going someplace without being attached to a pink rhinestone leash. Even in the doggie world that has to be totally humiliating!"

The girls led the dogs over to the newly created dog run, which backed up against the skateboarding area in the park. The run itself was a huge enclosed area with a fence running all around it so that any dogs inside could not escape, and some comfortable benches on which dog owners could rest. They carefully closed the gate behind them, reached down, and unleashed their dogs.

All of them, Tiffany included, started running together in big, happy circles.

"They like it," Cassie said happily as she sat down on one of the benches. Breezy and Annie sat down, too.

"You'd like it, too," Annie said, "if you were shut up inside all day, and got to go outside only three times, on a leash." She stretched her legs out in front of her and rested her hands on top of the baseball cap. "Now, *this* is more like my concept of working."

"Just be sure that Tiffany doesn't get overheated," Cassie warned.

Annie shot her a sideways look. "What is up with you? You act as if you actually like that snob Crystal."

"Well, she's a famous model," Cassie said. "I never knew anyone famous before."

"We treat everyone who hires us exactly the same," Breezy insisted, keeping her eyes on the dogs, who were happily chasing each other in the dog run. "Fame doesn't make any difference."

"You guys, didn't you notice something a little funny about Crystal being this big, famous model?" Annie asked.

Cassie shrugged. "Like what?"

"Like the fact that Crystal is short. She wears these stilts for shoes so that she'll look taller, but she's still short. Supermodels aren't short."

"Maybe some of them are and we just don't know about it," Cassie said.

"No," Annie insisted. "You have to be really tall, really skinny, really — "

"Hey, you guys, look over there!" Breezy interrupted, jutting her head toward a grove of trees on the other side of the dog run.

Across the fence, in the skateboarding area, David Silver and his friend Ben were practicing their Ollies and layback grinds on their skateboards.

"Your future husband is a pretty good skater," Annie teased Cassie.

"I don't want him to see me when I'm all sweaty from walking the dogs," Cassie said.

"You look fine," Breezy assured her. "Hey, look, the dogs went over to watch the guys skate."

Sure enough, all four dogs were standing at the fence, panting, their tails wagging, as they watched David and Ben execute their skateboard tricks. David stopped for a moment and reached his hand through the fence to pet Tiny. That's when he saw the girls and waved to them.

"Wave back!" Annie told Cassie as she waved at the guys.

"I can't even wave at him without feeling like an idiot," Cassie admitted, but she waved anyway.

"You don't need to feel so self-conscious now," Breezy reminded her. "I mean, he really did ask you to dance at Liza's wedding. And you said he was really nice to you last week when you went over to his house to see Melody."

"That's true, but — "

"Hey, look, the guys just took out their Frisbees," Annie said. "I think David is going to show off for you, Cassie."

David and Ben spread out and started throwing a Frisbee back and forth, their throws getting longer and longer, and their catches more and more acrobatic.

Annie stood up. "I'm gonna go play."

"You can't," Breezy said, casting a glance at the dogs, who were playfully wrestling with one another in the grass near the fence. "You're working."

"Who says . . . whoops!" Annie exclaimed as Ben let go with a mighty heave. But his toss was off-target, and the Frisbee flew crazily over the fenceline and into the dog run area.

"Wow, look at Tiffany!" Cassie exclaimed. The tiny poodle drew a bead on the flying Frisbee, raced after it, and then leaped a good two feet into the air to catch the plastic disc between her teeth.

"Awesome!" Annie shouted, jumping up and down. "Did you see that?" She turned to the dog. "Hey, Tiff, c'mere!"

The dog responded instantly to Annie's command and ran over to her, happily dropping the Frisbee at Annie's feet. Annie immediately picked it up, wound up, and threw the Frisbee expertly.

Tiffany ran right after it, waited for it to settle in the air about forty yards away from Annie, and then jumped to snare the Frisbee in midair.

"That's unbelievable!" Breezy marveled. "Where do you think she learned to do that?"

"Maybe she's just a natural athlete," Annie guessed. "A K-9 Frisbee dog!" She turned back to Tiffany and clapped her hands together. "Bring 'er here, big girl!"

The dog ran right back to Annie, dropped the Frisbee at her feet again, sat down, and looked up expectantly.

"This dog is da bomb!" Annie exclaimed. "I love her!" She knelt down and hugged the pink-tinged poodle. "I forgive you for looking so dorky," Annie told Tiffany. "That's the fault of dumb humans. What you need is a doggie makeover."

Cassie kept her eyes on Four-Oh-Nine, who

was cavorting in a circle with Minnie. "Crystal won't like it if we — "

"Hi."

Cassie looked up. It was David with Ben. She'd been so busy keeping her eye on the dogs that she hadn't noticed the guys come into the dog run.

"Hi," Cassie said shyly.

"Did you guys see that dog catch your disc?" Annie asked them. "How cool was that?"

"Whose dog is that?" Ben asked.

"Crystal Anders's," Breezy replied. "Crystal's mom hired us to take care of the dogs this week. Crystal's getting married soon, and — "

"You know Crystal Anders?" David interrupted.

"ABC Weddings is working on her wedding," Cassie explained.

Tiffany barked at David as if to ask him to throw the Frisbee again. David obliged, and Tiffany ran after it. "That means you guys will be at the barbecue that my mom is giving in honor of Crystal's wedding. Her mom and my mom play bridge together."

"I don't think we'll actually be invited," Breezy said. "I mean, Crystal used to be my baby-sitter when I was a little kid, but — "

"Mine too!" David said.

"No kidding?" Breezy marveled.

"She was the best," David recalled. "She used

226

to let me watch anything I wanted to watch on TV, and we used to play all these great video games together."

"I thought she was great, too," Breezy said. "But she's kind of . . . changed."

"Yeah, I heard she's this big model now or something," David said. He looked over at Cassie. "To tell you the truth, I kind of saw my mom's guest list. And you guys are all invited."

Cassie grinned. "That's so wonderful. We'd love to come!"

"I gotta see this girl Crystal," Ben said. "She's really a famous model, huh?"

"Maybe so and maybe not," Annie said mysteriously.

"Uh-oh, Four-Oh-Nine and Tiffany look like they're about to start fighting," Breezy said, hurrying over to the dogs.

"We've got to go anyway," Ben said.

"You can keep my Frisbee," David added. "For the superdog. So . . . I'll see you at the barbecue, Cassie."

"Great," Cassie replied happily.

As soon as the guys left, she clutched Annie's arm. "I have a date with David Silver!"

"It's not a *date*-date," Annie pointed out.

"Well, it's close," Cassie countered.

"Hey, Annie, grab Tiffany!" Breezy called as she headed back toward the girls.

But Annie didn't need to grab Tiffany, because the little dog ran right to her and jumped into her arms.

"Looks like you made a friend," Breezy said, laughing.

"Anyone — thing — that can play Frisbee like she does is my bud for life," Annie replied, giving Tiffany a big kiss.

"Let's round up the other dogs and head back," Breezy suggested.

As they walked to the other end of the dog run, with Tiffany still in Annie's arms, Cassie told Breezy all about her sort-of date with David. She went on and on about what she should wear and how she should act and how nervous she was already. When they reached the other dogs, they were happily romping around together, only they had a fourth dog with them. Reddish-haired, it looked like a combination of a dachshund and a beagle, with extremely soulful eyes and a funny-looking little tail.

"Now that is one goofy-looking dog," Annie said. She put Tiffany down and attached her dreaded pink leash. "I wonder whose he is."

Cassie looked around. "We're the only ones in the run."

They put leashes on Tiny, Minnie, and Four-Oh-Nine while the fourth dog stared at them, wagging his funny-looking tail.

Breezy knelt down and petted the dog. Then

she checked for a collar. "No collar," she reported.

"Let's check around the park and see if we can find the owner," Annie suggested.

"Good idea," Cassie said. "I can stay here with the dogs while you guys check, if you want."

"Just don't let any of them get away like last time," Annie reminded her.

Cassie sat on a bench, all the leashes firmly secured in her hand, while she thought about her upcoming sort-of date with David. *It will be the first date I've ever had,* she realized with a thrill. *And even though my parents won't let me date yet, they can't object to a barbecue in the Silvers' backyard, I don't think.*

A half hour later, Annie and Breezy came back. They had questioned every single person they could find in the park about the stray dog. No one had lost a dog and no one seemed to know the dog.

The lost dog had been sitting patiently near the four leashed canines. He went over to Cassie and licked her hand.

"We can't just leave him here," Cassie pleaded. "He's so . . . alone!"

Breezy thought for a moment. "I bet we could bring him to the clubhouse, for a while, anyway."

"Your mom will kill you," Annie said. "She wouldn't even let you have a gerbil."

"Maybe she'll be okay if it's just for a day or so."

"That's a great idea!" Cassie exclaimed as the stray rubbed itself against her chin. She bent down to scratch him behind the ears. "If we keep him in the clubhouse, we can take care of him until we find his owner."

"We can make signs and put them up," Annie suggested. "A hot dog like this has got to have an owner."

"That's it!" Cassie exclaimed. "We'll call him Hotdog!"

"He probably already has a name," Breezy cautioned.

"Hey, you like the name Hotdog, Hotdog?" Cassie asked. The dog replied by barking a couple of times and then rolling around happily on the ground in front of them while the other dogs watched him curiously.

"He likes it," Breezy surmised. "Okay, let's bring him home."

The procession that left the park was three girls and five dogs strong . . . four of them on leashes, and one of them cradled in Cassie's loving arms.

"Twenty-four hours," Mrs. Zeeman said firmly, looking first at Hotdog, who was greedily lapping up a bowl of milk the girls had brought up to the attic for him. "And not a single minute more. It's six-thirty now, so by tomorrow evening, he's someplace else."

"But Mom — " Breezy began.

"I'm sorry," Mrs. Zeeman said. "Your grandmother is allergic to dog hair, remember?"

"But Grandma is in Florida," Breezy reminded her mom.

"She comes to visit a lot," her mom said. "Twenty-four hours. I mean it."

"Okay," Breezy agreed reluctantly.

"Okay." Mrs. Zeeman turned toward the attic stairs and left the girls alone in the clubhouse. "The cardboard and markers you need to make those 'lost dog' signs are in the paper bag I brought up."

As Mrs. Zeeman left, Cassie looked over at Hotdog, who had just finished the bowl of milk.

"You want more, Hotdog?" Cassie asked.

Hotdog barked, so Cassie took the glass of milk she had been drinking and poured it into his bowl. He greedily finished that milk, too.

"Annie?" Cassie asked, looking pointedly at Annie's half-full glass.

"Oh, go ahead," Annie said, pushing the milk toward Cassie, who picked up the glass and poured it into Hotdog's bowl. He greedily lapped it up again. Then he looked expectantly at Cassie for more. Only there was no more.

That was when Hotdog started barking. And didn't stop.

Mrs. Zeeman came running up the stairs. As soon as she came into the attic, Hotdog quit barking and lay down on his side near the milk bowl.

"What is the problem?" Mrs. Zeeman asked.

"No problem," Breezy said sheepishly. "Hotdog was barking."

"Breezy, I'm trying to do my books. And I've got a ton of work I need to get done tonight for Crystal's wedding. You have to keep that dog quiet."

The instant Mrs. Zeeman went out of the room, the dog started barking again.

"He only shuts up for your mom," Cassie realized.

"I think we're going to have to ask your mother to be a member of the club," Annie said. "Either that, or get earplugs."

"Give him my peanut butter cookies," Breezy pleaded. "Anything to get him to be quiet." She tossed a few cookies at the dog. Although they shattered into several pieces on the floor, Hotdog chowed them down.

"Well, one thing's for sure," Annie said.

"What's that?" Cassie asked.

"The dog will eat anything. And when he's chewing, he isn't barking. Which means that the three of us are going to be making a permanent raid on the refrigerator until we find Hotdog a home!"

28

"Now, Breezy," Mrs. Anders said, her voice on the phone rising. "I don't want that new dog to take up any more of you girls' time."

"Yes, Mrs. Anders," Breezy replied, looking over at Hotdog, who was fast asleep on the attic pillow where Cassie usually hung out.

"Because I hired you girls to take care of my Crystal's little Tiffany, not some stray animal you came across in the park."

"Yes, Mrs. Anders."

Hotdog rolled over and stretched.

He is incredibly cute, Breezy thought. *I wish I could keep him.*

"And my Crystal is getting very, very upset," Mrs. Anders went on. "It's enough that Annie is turning Tiffany into some, some Frisbee fiend! I don't think my Crystal should be upset during the last week before her wedding, do you?"

"Yes, Mrs. . . . I mean not at all, Mrs. Anders," Breezy answered.

"You girls have had that dog for a week now, correct?"

"That's right."

"So now you'll do what you told me about, right?"

"Right, Mrs. Anders."

"Good," Mrs. Anders said. "And then you girls will stop by afterwards? There's some last-minute planning I need to go over with you. The barbecue is just the day after tomorrow, remember."

"We'll be there," Breezy promised as Hotdog walked over to the attic window and peered out into the late-afternoon sunshine.

"Then we'll see you later," Mrs. Anders said. "Good-bye, Breezy."

Breezy said good-bye, and Mrs. Anders hung up. Hotdog lay back down by the window, rolled over, and stretched languidly once again.

Breezy looked at the dog and sighed. It was a week after she and her friends had found Hotdog, and despite their best efforts, they had had no luck at all in finding the funny-looking dog's owners.

ABC Weddings had made and put posters up all over Summerville — it seemed as if there were more posters on telephone poles about Hotdog than there were about ABC Weddings. They'd even managed to enlist David and Ben to put up some signs, going up and down Summerville's main shopping street and asking merchants to put the posters in the windows. Hotdog was the best-known dog in Summerville.

But it was no use. No one had called to claim the dog.

So Hotdog had stayed in the attic clubhouse, day after day. Breezy and her friends had taken him out whenever they went over to take care of Tiffany and the other three dogs, but the fact of the matter was, Hotdog was, well, difficult.

He had an unbelievable appetite.

He barked a lot.

He decided to create a game for himself in the attic by seeing how many things he could knock over in one mad dash through.

Finally, Mrs. Zeeman had laid down the law.

"I said he could stay here one day," she'd told Breezy. "Not seven days. Brianna Zeeman, you will take that dog to the shelter."

And that's what Breezy was going to do. Right now.

"C'mere, Hotdog," Breezy said, calling to the dog.

Obediently, he trotted over and curled up at Breezy's feet.

A sob caught in Breezy's throat.

Well, he's adoptable, she thought as she got to her feet. She had arranged to meet Cassie and Annie at the animal shelter later, since the two of them were busy with the other four dogs and had asked Breezy to spend the afternoon with Hotdog.

"Okay, Hotdog," Breezy said as she fastened the leash to the collar her mom had bought for the dog. "Let's go out there and find someone to give you a great home."

"I've never been inside here," Cassie admitted as the three members of ABC Weddings stood outside the stark metal door of the Summerville Animal Shelter. She was holding Hotdog in her arms.

"Me neither," Annie said, regarding the door dubiously.

"It doesn't look very pleasant," Breezy commented, but she pressed the buzzer anyway.

The door swung open automatically. Inside, it looked more like a doctor's waiting room than what they'd thought an animal shelter might look like. There was even a young woman wearing hospital-type scrubs sitting at a desk behind a glass window.

Breezy hesitated a moment and then led her friends over to the woman.

"May I help you?" the woman asked. She had a nameplate that read VOLUNTEER: MARIE.

"We have a dog," Breezy said.

"I can see that," Marie replied.

The girls were all silent. None of them could bring themselves to say that they wanted to leave Hotdog here at the shelter. They each knew that they had homes to go to. Hotdog, though, had no home.

"Do you need to place this dog for adoption?" Marie asked.

All three girls nodded solemnly.

"Is this dog a pet?" Marie asked.

"Oh, no!" Cassie said. "We found him in the park a week ago — "

"And we took care of him for a week — " Breezy added.

"But our parents say we can't keep him," Annie finished. "But he's really, really nice. His name is Hotdog."

"Can you find him a home?" Cassie asked, her eyes wide.

"Just a minute," Marie said. The girls watched as she got up from behind her desk and walked out of her office and into the waiting area, picking up a clipboard on the way.

"Now," Marie said, "let's sit down and talk."

Quickly and efficiently, Marie took down all kinds of information about Breezy, at whose home Hotdog had stayed, and about the dog himself. She was particularly interested in the way that the girls had found him, and as they recounted the story of how they'd found him in the park, Marie shook her head.

"People should never treat animals like that," she said solemnly.

"We agree, Marie," Cassie said. "Now, do you think you can find him a home?"

Marie sighed and reached down to stroke Hotdog, who had gotten comfortable at their feet. "I certainly hope so."

"But you're not sure," Annie challenged.

"We can't ever be sure," Marie said. "And with the deadline so short these days . . ." Her voice trailed off.

The deadline so short? Breezy thought. *Whatever could that mean?*

And then she figured it out.

"How long will you keep Hotdog before you put him to sleep?" Breezy asked Marie.

Cassie gasped. Even Annie looked surprised. Neither of them had really considered this a possibility.

Marie looked at them closely, and then down at Hotdog.

"Because of recent funding cuts for the shelter," she said, her voice suddenly getting very official-sounding, "our mandate is to hold animals for adoption for a period of forty-eight hours."

"Forty-eight hours!" Annie exploded. "That's just two days!"

Marie's eyes stayed on Hotdog. "I'm sorry. It's the best we can do."

"It's not very good," Cassie said, tears pooling in her eyes.

"Like I said," Marie repeated, "I'm sorry. We'd

like to keep the animals longer. My best advice to you is, try to find a home for this dog if you have to leave him with us. And the sooner you do it, the better."

"No, no, no," Mrs. Anders said. "It's completely out of the question."

"But Hotdog will die if you don't," Cassie pleaded. "You have a big house."

"Cassie, I am not interested in adopting that, that . . . mutt," Mrs. Anders said, rising to her feet from the chair at the kitchen table. The three members of ABC Weddings were at the table as well. "Now, what would you like to talk about here, that animal, or my Crystal's wedding, for which you were hired to help?"

It was an hour and a half later, and the sad trio that was ABC Weddings had gone over to Mrs. Anders's house as scheduled. But on the way, they had revowed that they were going to find a good home for Hotdog, no matter what.

"No way is that dog gonna die," Annie had said. "Not so long as I'm alive."

That's why they'd spent the first ten minutes of their meeting with Mrs. Anders trying to talk her into adopting Hotdog. And they would have done the same thing with Crystal, too, except she was in Indianapolis taking in a play at the famous Phoenix Theatre.

It made no difference. Crystal already had

Tiffany, and Mrs. Anders wasn't interested in Hotdog, no matter how good a sales job ABC Weddings did about the stray dog.

"The wedding," Cassie said meekly.

"Absolutely," Breezy added, trying to be as professional as possible.

"Good," Mrs. Anders said. "I have something to show you." She walked out of the kitchen for a moment, and then came back in carrying three matching black-and-white-checkered shirts, and matching black-and-white-checkered aprons.

Cassie thought they were some of the most awful-looking garments she had ever seen in her life.

"What are those?" she asked.

"For you girls," Mrs. Anders said. "For the barbecue. Since this is Indianapolis, I thought we'd go with an Indy 500 racing theme. I love the checkered aprons."

"Uh, Mrs. Anders?" Annie asked, eyeing the aprons suspiciously. "If David Silver's mother is giving this barbecue for Crystal, and we girls are invited, then what do we have to have aprons for?"

There was a moment of dead silence, and then Mrs. Anders started to laugh. And she laughed for a good five seconds.

"My word, Annie," she said. "You have a wonderful sense of humor."

"Huh?" Annie asked.

Mrs. Anders smiled. "These clothes are for you girls. Wear them with black pants, please. Since you're going to be serving at the barbecue, I want you looking spiffy."

"Spiffy," Breezy repeated dully. She looked at Cassie, whose face was a mask of sheer horror.

Cassie had figured it out quickly this time.

If she was going to be serving at the Silvers' barbecue for Crystal and her fiancé, Tom, that meant there was a really good chance of something unbelievably horrible happening.

She was, without a doubt, going to be David Silver's *waitress*.

29

"Cassie, bring out some more coleslaw, please!"

"Yes, Mrs. Anders," Cassie said as she set down a huge tray of canned soft drinks she'd brought out from the Silvers' kitchen. She bent down to tie her sneaker.

"Now, Cassie," Mrs. Anders said, her hands on her hips. "The guests don't have any food."

Cassie looked at the fifty or so people who had gathered in the Silvers' backyard. They were eating, chatting, or playing lawn darts. A small crowd, including David and Ben, had gathered around a miniature slot-car track that Mr. Silver had erected on a large worktable, in keeping with the party's Indy 500 theme, and were racing tiny slot cars around and around it.

Everyone has food, Cassie thought belligerently. *Everyone is having fun. Everyone has on decent outfits, too. Everyone but me, that is.*

She stomped back into the kitchen, almost colliding with Breezy, who had on the identical horrid black-and-white-checked garments. "Mrs. Anders wants more coleslaw," she reported.

"There's another tub on the kitchen table," Breezy said. "Are you okay?"

"No, I'm not okay," Cassie said. She took off the ridiculous-looking black-and-white-checked hat and smoothed her hair back. "David has hardly said two words to me, and I look like an idiot in this outfit."

Annie came into the house carrying a nearly empty bowl of potato salad. "I heard that. If it makes you feel any better, all three of us look like idiots in these outfits."

"It doesn't," Cassie said, sighing.

"You'll have another chance to have a first date with David," Breezy said sympathetically. "I'm sure of it."

"I'm not. David's ignoring me," Cassie reported.

"I was just talking to Crystal's fiancé, Tom, outside." Annie said. "He's such a nice guy. He's a huge Cubs fan. What could he possibly see in her?"

"She's a big model," Cassie explained. "Lots of guys want to date models."

"Cassie, in this lifetime?" Mrs. Anders called, referring to the coleslaw. "Annie, I need you to make more guacamole. And Breezy, the dishwasher needs filling again."

"I hate this job," Cassie muttered, and hurried to work. Her friends weren't far behind.

"This is the fifth time I've loaded this dishwasher," Breezy said.

"I'll come back in and help you after I get rid of this," Cassie said as she went outside with the coleslaw.

"How much are we getting paid for doing this, again?" Annie asked, reaching for the ripe avocados and a fork.

"A lot," Breezy replied.

"It's not enough, however much it is." Annie peeled an avocado and dropped the sticky green mess into the bowl. "Hasn't Mrs. Silver ever heard of a food processor?"

"She said it's broken," Breezy explained. She rinsed off some glasses and put them into the dishwasher. "I keep thinking that instead of being in here working, we should be out there asking people if they'll adopt Hotdog. But then I feel guilty, because I know I'm supposed to be in here working."

"Hotdog is more important than this barbecue," Annie said. "I got to talk to a few people when I went around cleaning up before. So far no luck, though."

"David just talked to me," Cassie reported as she came back inside.

"What did he say?" Breezy asked.

"He asked if there were any cold cans of Coke," Cassie said with disgust.

"Go pour one on his head," Annie suggested.

"He wasn't being mean," Cassie admitted, sitting down at the kitchen table. "I think he was just trying to think of something to say to me. He asked me about Hotdog, too. I told him we still haven't found him a home."

"We've got to find some way to save his life," Breezy insisted, sitting down next to Cassie.

"Sometimes I just hate being a kid," Annie said, leaning against the wall. "I mean, if I were an adult, no one could tell me I couldn't keep Hotdog. How come adults get all the power?"

No one had an answer for that.

"Once this barbecue is over, we're still going to see Hotdog at the shelter, right?" Cassie asked.

Annie nodded in agreement. "The shelter closes at nine. We have to make sure we get out of here in time."

"Before . . . " Breezy began. But she couldn't finish. It was just too awful to say, before they put Hotdog to sleep.

"Cassie!" Mrs. Anders said, striding into the kitchen. "Where are those baked beans?"

Cassie stood up quickly. "You didn't tell me to put out more baked beans, Mrs. Anders."

"I distinctly remember telling you . . . never mind. Just do it, please. And girls, the big toast to the bridal couple is in just a few minutes. You can come outside and take a short break then." She turned on her heel and went back to the party.

"Mrs. Anders never seems to remember what she told us and what she didn't tell us," Cassie said. She reached for a vat of baked beans on the counter. "See you guys."

The baked beans were really heavy, so Cassie was walking quickly so she could get them out to the large serving table. But just as she was walking out, Mrs. Anders was walking in, and the two of them bumped into each other.

Cassie did her best to keep her balance. The vat of beans wavered in her hands. She readjusted her weight to keep the beans from falling, which made her fall instead. Right on her butt.

The vat of baked beans landed with her, all over her.

And of course, David Silver was standing right there, watching the whole thing.

"I'm cursed," Cassie said as she stood in the bathroom while her two friends tried to help wash the beans off of her. "Whenever I'm around David, I'm cursed. First I land in a mud pile. Now this!"

"It's not that bad," Annie told her. "It was an accident."

It was ten minutes later, and all three girls were temporarily off-duty, waiting for the big exchange of toasts that was to celebrate the wedding party. Cassie had been so mortified that when David had tried to help her up she wouldn't even let him take her hand. And she hadn't seen him since. She was pretty sure she never wanted to see him again.

"Well, that looks a lot better," Breezy said, eyeing Cassie. "Your outfit is still a little brown, but it's okay."

"I'm staying in this bathroom forever," Cassie decided.

There was a knock on the bathroom door. "Excuse me in there! I need to use the ladies' room!" a voice called in.

"Well, so much for your hiding place," Annie said. "Let's go face the music."

The girls wandered into the kitchen.

"Say cheese, gang!" a male voice said from behind them. They turned around to find Tom Logan smiling at them, a camera up to his eyes. More cameras hung around his neck. The auto-advance on his camera whirred as he clicked off some shots of the girls.

"I'm not exactly at my best," Cassie explained shyly.

"The three of you are darling," Tom insisted. He took another shot. "If you give me your address, Breezy, I'll send you and your friends some prints."

"Great," Breezy said.

Crystal came into the kitchen. "Tom, everyone wants to know why you aren't outside," she said imperiously.

"Because I'm in here, taking shots of these cuties," he explained.

"This is not a photo shoot, okay?" she said coldly. "This is a party in honor of us."

"Uh, excuse us," Breezy muttered, and the three girls tiptoed outside.

"He's nice and cute, so I can't figure out what he's doing with Crystal the Model Witch," Annie said when they got outside.

Breezy nodded in agreement. "Why would a guy that nice marry someone who isn't nice at all?"

"Maybe she's nice in private," Cassie suggested.

"Breezy, dear," Mrs. Anders said, hurrying over to the girls, "I left some notes for my toast on the table in the dining room. Be a dear and get them for me."

"I'll come with you," Annie offered.

"Me too," Cassie said glumly. "David's talking to some people I don't even know."

The three girls went back inside. But from the hallway, before they got to the dining room, they heard Tom's and Crystal's raised voices.

"Oh, come on, Crystal, they're just kids. I think they're cute," Tom said.

"I guess that's why you were in here taking photos of them," Crystal snapped.

"What's wrong with being nice and paying some attention to them?" Tom replied. "We were kids once, too. It wasn't that long ago."

"They're small-town girls. I know all about small-town girls, remember? I grew up here. Those girls are probably just as snotty as the girls I grew up with, the ones who said I wasn't cute enough to make it as a model. Besides, they're the hired help."

The girls looked at one another. They could hardly believe what they were hearing.

"Crystal," Tom said, and the girls could hear his voice get lower. It was full of love. "I love you. I know some bad stuff happened here when you were a kid. But you're not a kid anymore. You don't have to put on this big act in front of all these people."

"That shows how much you know about a small town," Crystal said coldly. "They'd all just love to hear that I failed as a model."

"But you haven't failed," Tom said. "Just because you're too short for fashion doesn't mean you haven't done a lot of good work. Look at all the print ads you've done — "

"No one cares about that," Crystal said sadly. "I'm a big failure."

"That's why you pretend you work with top

models like Claudia Schiffer and Linda Evange-lista," Tom said kindly.

"How do you know I — "

"I heard you," Tom said.

"Girls!" Mrs. Anders said, hurrying over to them. "Why are you standing here in the hall? I just asked you to get my notes!"

"We didn't want to interrupt a private conversation in the dining room," Breezy explained. "Crystal and Tom were talking."

"Oh, believe me, my Crystal doesn't keep anything from her mother," Mrs. Anders said, hurrying into the dining room.

The girls went outside and huddled together under a large oak tree.

"She's not a top model," Cassie said. "She's not famous at all."

"Well, that explains everything," Breezy commented. "Tom's right. She's insecure, so she has to act like she's better than everyone."

"Who cares why she's doing it?" Annie said, taking a piece of bubble gum out of her pocket and putting it in her mouth. "She's still doing it. And it doesn't help us with our biggest problem."

"Hotdog?" Cassie asked.

Annie looked down at her watch. "It's seven o'clock now," she said. "We don't have much time."

The girls rolled their bikes to a stop in front of the animal shelter. They climbed off, took off their helmets, and unstrapped their riding lights from their legs as quickly as they could.

On the bike ride over, they had discussed what Breezy had called Operation Hotdog. No way were they going to let Hotdog die.

"Follow me," Breezy instructed. "Just do what I do."

Together, the three girls went up to the door of the shelter and rang the buzzer. It opened immediately, and Marie, dressed in the same hospital-type scrubs as the last time, opened the door for them.

"Girls!" she said happily. "You're back."

"We had to come back, Marie," Breezy said.

"I'm hoping you found a home for Hotdog," Marie said.

"Not exactly," Breezy admitted.

Marie's face fell. "I'm so sorry. I guess you wanted to see Hotdog one last time. But won't that make it even harder for you?"

"We thought we could take him for a walk," Annie said.

"A short walk," Cassie added.

Breezy gave Marie a very direct look and hoped her plan would work. "The thing with Hotdog is, sometimes a short walk turns into a long walk. A really long walk."

The girls waited, holding their breath. Marie thought a moment, then she spoke.

"I'll get Hotdog for you," she said. "Remember

that the doors to the shelter will be locked in fifteen minutes. And if a dog isn't back by then . . . then he isn't back." She walked away to get the dog.

"She knows," Cassie whispered to her friends.

"Well, we aren't allowed to adopt him because we're kids," Breezy said. "We'd have to have a parent with us. And we all know none of our parents are going to let us adopt him. So . . . we're going to do what we have to do."

Cassie and Annie nodded, their faces serious.

Breezy nodded, too. "We're going to dog-nap him."

30

"That's okay, Melissa. Thanks anyway."

Breezy hung up the phone and sighed. Melissa Beasley was a girl in her class whose parents owned a pet store. Breezy thought maybe Melissa's parents would agree that Melissa could adopt Hotdog. But Melissa's parents wouldn't even consider it. They said their house was already a menagerie.

Breezy had made fifteen calls in the past hour, trying to find Hotdog a home. She'd had no luck at all. She picked up his favorite rubber dog bone and threw it to him, and watched as Hotdog slobbered all over his toy. The girls had bought him quite a few toys in the past sixteen hours.

Sixteen hours. That's how long it had been since Breezy and her friends had snuck Hotdog back into the attic clubhouse. Amazingly enough, so far her parents hadn't found the dog. Luck had been on her side. Her dad had been at a seminar in Indianapolis for his accounting business, and her mom was so busy with both Crystal's wedding and another wedding the very next week that she was hardly ever home.

However, her good luck was about to run out.

Crystal's wedding was tomorrow. Her dad would return from his seminar tomorrow, and he always stored his seminar materials in a closet in the attic. And Breezy still had no home for Hotdog.

"I've just got to think of something," Breezy told the dog. He stopped chewing on his bone long enough to cock his head at her in an endearing fashion. She got down on her knees and laid her head next to Hotdog's. "I won't let you die, Hotdog, no matter what."

Hotdog barked once in agreement.

"Breezy!" her mom called up the attic steps.

Oh, no! Her mom was home. She hadn't thought her mother would get home until that evening. Quickly she ran down the stairs so that her mother wouldn't come up and find the dog.

"Hi, Mom," Breezy said.

"Hi, sweetie." Her mom was at the kitchen table, looking through some mail. "Did your sister call?"

"No," Breezy reported, sitting next to her mother. "But I guess you can't expect her to call all that much from her honeymoon."

"You're right," her mother agreed. "But that

doesn't stop me from asking mother-type questions. Such as, did you eat any lunch?"

"I had a sandwich," Breezy said.

"Once Grandma gets here tomorrow, I promise I'll be home more," Mrs. Zeeman said. "Speaking of Grandma, I left a bunch of old photos in a box up in the attic that I promised I'd get for her. She wants to make them into albums for us."

Uh-oh. That meant her mother had to get into the attic.

Today.

"I could get them for you, Mom," Breezy offered quickly.

"Oh, no, sweetie, that's okay. I know how busy you are. Aren't you girls supposed to be getting Tiffany groomed today and then taking the dog to the photo shoot at the church?"

"Annie and Cassie are at the groomers with Tiffany right now," Breezy reported. "Then they're stopping here to get me and we're all going to the church together."

Mrs. Zeeman got up and put the teakettle on to boil. "How did you get out of going to the groomers?"

Breezy couldn't tell the truth — that they had all decided that while Cassie and Annie had Tiffany at the groomers, Breezy would make another round of phone calls to everyone she knew in a last-ditch attempt to find Hotdog a home.

"The groomer really didn't need three people waiting around for Tiffany," Breezy said. She got up and got a glass from the cupboard, and poured herself a glass of milk while her mom made herself a cup of tea. "Is everything ready for Crystal's wedding tomorrow?"

"Just about," Mrs. Zeeman said. She sat back down and took a sip of her tea. "Have you noticed that Mrs. Anders is just a tad difficult to work with? She's forever asking why something hasn't been done, and it invariably turns out to be something we never discussed."

"She does that to you, too?" Breezy asked, laughing.

"All the time," her mom replied.

The doorbell rang. "I'm sure that's Annie and Cassie," Breezy said, running to get it. Cassie and Annie stood at the door with Tiffany in Annie's arms. The poodle's fur was now lavender, as were her nails. Parts of her were almost bald, and she had lavender bows in the puffballs that had been sculpted from what was left of her coat. She even had lavender rhinestone studs on her ears.

"Look what they did to Tiff," Annie said sorrowfully.

Breezy looked more closely. "Oh, my gosh, did they actually pierce her ears?"

"No," Cassie said. "They use some kind of dog-friendly adhesive to keep the earrings on. Mrs. Garaway, the groomer, had to follow Crystal's exact directions for Tiffany's grooming. I could tell she thought it was ridiculous."

"Can you imagine doing that to this terrific Frisbee-catcher?" Annie asked, looking down at Tiffany. "It's a crime."

From inside the house, Breezy heard the phone ring. She looked behind her quickly to make sure her mom wasn't within hearing distance. She leaned closer to her friends.

"Listen, you guys, my mom is going up to the attic later this afternoon to get some old photos. We've got to smuggle Hotdog out of there."

"I saw your mom's car," Cassie said conspiratorially. "We're just lucky she hasn't caught Hotdog already."

"I know," Breezy agreed. "Good thing we found out that as long as Hotdog has food, he doesn't bark. I feed him all the time to keep him quiet. Last night my mom saw that all the cold barbecued chicken she had left in the fridge was gone. I told her I had been really, really hungry. She said, 'For an entire chicken?' "

"Tell her it's because you're weaning yourself off junk food," Cassie suggested.

"So, how are we going to get Hotdog out of the house?" Annie asked, putting Tiffany down. The little dog rubbed lovingly against Annie's leg.

"I haven't figured that out yet," Breezy admitted. "Help me think."

"Well, we'd better think of something fast,"

Annie said, "because we're supposed to have Tiff over at the church for photos in a half hour."

"Breezy?" Mrs. Zeeman asked, hurrying over to her daughter, her purse over her arm. She seemed very harried. "The caterer for Crystal's wedding just called. It seems three of her employees decided to try the salmon mousse for tomorrow and they all got violently ill. I have to go over there and find out what's going on before we poison everyone."

"Oh, good," Breezy said without thinking, since it meant they'd be able to sneak Hotdog out of the house as soon as her mom left. Then she realized how that sounded. "I meant, oh, good, you found out about the salmon before the wedding," she added hastily.

"I have to run," Mrs. Zeeman said, kissing Breezy on the forehead. "Do you girls want a ride over to the church?"

"Oh, no, we'll bike over," Annie said. "I'll just put Tiffany in the basket on my bike."

"Cute," Mrs. Zeeman said. "Well, I'm off. And listen, I want you girls to know that Paula and I both think you're doing a great job. It's a huge help to us."

"Thanks, Mom," Breezy said.

As her mom hurried to her car, Annie tied Tiffany's leash to the rocking chair on the front porch. Then the three girls hurried up to the attic. Hotdog was thrilled to see all three of them.

He immediately jumped all over them, dancing around with happiness.

"Yes, we love you, too, you big Hotdog," Annie said, ruffling Hotdog's fur.

"I don't suppose you had any luck with your phone calls," Cassie asked Breezy as Breezy attached Hotdog's leash.

"You suppose right," Breezy said sadly. "As of right now, we have no home for Hotdog."

"But we have to do something," Cassie insisted.

"I know that," Breezy agreed. "But for once I'm all out of ideas. You guys, I don't know what we're going to do."

31

"I hope Mrs. Anders doesn't get all crazy when we show up at the church with Tiffany and Hotdog," Cassie said, watching as Hotdog turned over onto his back so Breezy could scratch his stomach.

"Well, we're not going to be dumb enough to bring the supermutt into the church," Annie said.

Breezy looked at her watch. "We'd better hurry." Hotdog looked at her expectantly, wagging his tail. "Look at him. He totally trusts me. How can I let him down?"

She knelt down to the dog. "Yes, Hotdog, we're going out!"

Hotdog barked with joy and rushed over to the stairs, dragging Breezy with him. When Tiffany and Hotdog saw each other, they both did some serious sniffing, and then they wanted to play. But Annie picked up the toy poodle and put her in the basket of her bike. Breezy held tightly to Hotdog's leash, and the happy dog trotted along as the three girls slowly pedaled their way to the nearby church.

Tom Logan was in front of the church when the girls arrived, taking shots of the stained-glass windows. He looked very handsome in jeans and a white linen shirt. The girls knew the plan was for the wedding photographer to take some family shots today during the wedding rehearsal, to reduce the number she'd have to take tomorrow.

Tom smiled when he saw them, then gave a bemused look at Breezy, who was leading the funny-looking Hotdog on his leash. "You girls seem to have one too many dogs with you."

"This one is only along for the ride," Breezy explained as she got off her bike.

"He's kind of cute . . . in a bizarre way," Tom said, kneeling down to scratch Hotdog under the chin.

"I hope Crystal and Mrs. Anders won't be mad that Hotdog came with us," Cassie said. "I mean, we know we're working now, but — "

"Not to worry," Tom assured her. "My lips are sealed."

Breezy quickly tied Hotdog to a fence that bordered the front of the church. "Is everyone inside?"

"Most of the wedding party, both families, and a photographer," Tom said. "She's snapping portraits of Crystal first. You might want to get Tiff inside, though, in case Crystal wants pictures of her holding the pooch." He looked dubiously down at Tiffany. "She's kind of a scary color, don't you think?"

The girls laughed and led Tiffany on her leash into the church. About twenty people were milling around the church lobby, sipping punch or eating tiny sandwiches from a small buffet table. Crystal's brother, Pete, was flirting with a beautiful girl in the corner. Annie's mother was putting more sandwiches out as one of the Perfect Weddings employees cleaned up the used plates and cups.

"Hi, Mom," Annie said. "How's it going?"

"It's going," Mrs. McGee said, clearly distracted. "I hope I brought enough sandwiches."

Anxious as usual, Annie thought. She patted her mom's arm. "I'm sure you're doing great."

"Girls, go right in," Mrs. Anders said, hurrying over to them. "My Crystal needs her Tiffany right away."

Crystal was in the sanctuary, posing for the photographer. The photographer's assistant reset the lights while a makeup artist blotted the shine from Crystal's face. Crystal wore a long, flowing, lavender and white floral-print silk dress, and posed in front of a huge arrangement of pink and lavender flowers.

"Tiffany!" Crystal cried when she saw the girls with her dog. "Give me my baby girl!"

Annie handed over the dog, who whined pitifully at her separation from her new favorite human, Annie.

"What's wrong with her?" Crystal asked anxiously.

"Nothing," Annie said. "She just likes me."

"You haven't been feeding her meat, have you?" Crystal asked. "Because she only cries when her stomach is upset."

"Shall we go on with the shoot?" the photographer asked.

"I'd like some portraits of me with Tiffany," Crystal said. "And then some portraits of me and Tom."

"The dog just got billing over me," Tom said, his eyes twinkling.

"Oh, I didn't mean it like that," Crystal assured him. "Girls, wait in the lobby. I'll call you when I need you to get Tiffany."

The girls wandered back into the lobby and got some punch. At that moment, David Silver walked into the church, holding his little sister's hand. Cassie almost dropped her punch glass.

"Cassie!" Melody cried, running over to her and throwing her arms around her. "I didn't know you would be here!"

"Well, I didn't know you would be here, either," Cassie said, hugging the little girl back. "Are you in Crystal's wedding?"

Melody shook her head no. "But I was away at Grandma's when Mommy and Daddy gave a party for Crystal, so Crystal said I could come over here for this party. She's so nice."

Cassie, Annie, and Breezy exchanged looks. Melody thought Crystal was *nice*?

"She sends me dolls from New York sometimes," Melody said, holding on to Cassie's hand. "She's so pretty. She's as pretty as the dolls she sends me. I don't like her better than you, though."

Cassie smiled. "I'm honored."

"Yeah, I remember that word!" Melody said. She looked at her big brother. "David is honored, too!" She put her hand over her mouth and giggled, then she ran over to the entrance to the sanctuary and peeked in at the ongoing photo shoot.

Annie and Breezy made some excuse about wanting to get some food at the small buffet so they could leave David and Cassie alone.

"I was baby-sitting, so I had to bring the kid over," David explained. He put his hands in his pockets. "So, how's it going?"

"Okay," Cassie said. She had totally not expected to see David there, and she was glad that since she knew they were going to be inside the church, she had worn cute orange and pink rayon pants and a matching shirt instead of her usual cutoffs.

He scratched his chin. "So . . . you guys ended

264

264

up working really hard at that barbecue, huh?"

"Uh-huh."

"Yeah, it seemed like it," David said. "So, I guess you didn't get to have too much fun, then."

"It was okay," Cassie replied.

David scuffed his shoe against the floor. "Well, maybe a bunch of us could, like, go hang out at Wagner Lake Park. You know, play Frisbee, have a picnic, swim . . . since you didn't get to have any fun at the barbecue, I mean."

Cassie flushed with happiness. "That sounds like fun," she said shyly, proud of herself for managing to give a coherent answer.

"Excuse me," the photographer's assistant said, sticking her head into the lobby. "We need Pete, Mr. and Mrs. Anders, and the Logan family inside now, please. And Crystal asked ABC Weddings to come in and watch Tiffany and help with the flower girl and the ring bearer, please."

"I'm working," Cassie explained to David.

"I'll be out here waiting," David said. "No way can I drag Melody away before the whole shoot is done. She's in heaven."

"So, I guess I'll see you after, then," Cassie said.

For the next hour, Annie, Breezy, and Cassie entertained Tiffany, Crystal's five-year-old cousin, Wendy Anders, and Tom's four-year-old nephew, Michael Logan, as the photographer shot endless photos. Finally it was over, and Mrs. Anders told the girls to take Tiffany back to Pete's house.

"We'd better leave quickly," Breezy told her friends.

"Yeah, let's see if we can make the great escape before we have to explain Hotdog to Mrs. Anders," Annie agreed.

Cassie saw David near the food table talking sports with another cousin of Tom's, and she said good-bye quickly.

"I could call you about that picnic, maybe," David said casually, unable to look Cassie in the eye.

"That would be great," Cassie told him. "Where's Melody?"

"She's in the ladies' room with Crystal," David said.

"Tell her I said bye." Cassie hurried out front to meet her friends, almost flying from happiness. "You guys aren't going to believe what just happened — " Then she noticed the panicked look on Breezy's and Annie's faces. "What happened?"

"Don't you notice anything strange?" Annie asked, her voice tight with anxiety. Tiffany barked once and licked Annie's face to try and comfort her.

"What?" Cassie asked, looking around. Then she realized. "Where's Hotdog?"

"That's what we want to know," Breezy said. "When we got out here, Hotdog was gone."

"Gone?" Cassie echoed. "But he was tied to the fence."

"Well, he either got free or someone untied him," Annie said, worry etched across her face.

"We've got to look for him," Breezy said, almost in tears. "We've got to find him!"

"But we've got to get Tiffany back to Pete's house," Cassie reminded her. "We're working."

"Too bad," Breezy said. "If we take Tiffany back, by the time we get back here, who knows how far away Hotdog could be?"

Annie and Cassie looked at each other. They had never seen Breezy like this before. She was always the first one to make sure she did everything perfectly.

"How about if I take Tiff to the house while you guys look for Hotdog," Annie offered. "I'll come right back here and meet up with you."

They agreed on the plan, and when David came out of the church with Melody, they enlisted his help. Fortunately, Mrs. Anders was so scattered about the wedding that she didn't protest when she saw that all three girls hadn't departed with the poodle.

For the next hour, Breezy, Cassie, David, and Melody looked for Hotdog. When Annie got back, she joined them in the search for another hour.

They went to the park and looked in the dog run, went by the middle school and the high school, and biked down every street they could, calling out for the dog until their voices were hoarse.

They looked everywhere, and found nothing.

Breezy's heart was breaking. The funny-looking dog with no home, whom she had come to love, seemed to have disappeared into thin air.

32

"**B**reezy, you look just beautiful," her mother said as she stood in the doorway of Breezy's bedroom.

"Thanks, Mom," Breezy said, trying to muster up some enthusiasm. She had on the dress she was wearing to Crystal's wedding that afternoon, a pale blue jumper with a short-sleeved sweater underneath. She had picked it out herself at the mall, and she'd even chipped in some money to buy it, using some of what she'd earned from ABC Weddings. But now all the joy had gone out of the new outfit, because Hotdog was still missing. Breezy didn't think she'd ever see him again.

Mrs. Zeeman felt her daughter's forehead. "Are you okay, honey? Are you sick?"

"I'm fine, Mom," Breezy said. She knew how depressed she sounded, but she just couldn't help it. And she couldn't very well tell her mother the truth — that she had deliberately disobeyed her, lied to her, in fact, by sneaking Hotdog back into the clubhouse.

"Are Annie and Cassie meeting you here?" Mrs. Zeeman asked.

At that moment, Annie and Cassie stuck their heads into Breezy's room. They, too, were all dressed up. Annie wore a long floral-print skirt and a white blouse, and she had left her beloved baseball cap at home. Cassie sported a new outfit her mom had found for her in Indianapolis. It was pale pink velvet with cap sleeves and a swirly skirt that fell to a few inches above her knees. But even though the girls looked really pretty, their faces were as long as Breezy's.

Mrs. Zeeman studied them. "Something's bothering all of you," she decided, "and don't tell me I'm imagining things."

"There are some things you can't tell your mom, even when you have a great one," Breezy said.

Mrs. Zeeman smiled sadly. "You're growing up, honey. I guess I can't expect you to confide everything to me anymore." She kissed Breezy on the forehead. "I can drop you girls at the church if you like, before I run over to the country club."

"My mom went over there two hours ago," Annie reported, rolling her eyes. "She has six copies of her 'to do' list stashed in different places, just in case."

"She's thorough," Mrs. Zeeman agreed. "So, how about a ride?"

"Sure," Cassie replied. "That is, if you don't mind having Tiffany in your car."

"After all the time that dog spends at the groomer's, she's probably cleaner than all of us," Mrs. Zeeman said.

Breezy's dad stuck his head into the room. "Hey, all you girls look really great," he said, smiling. "Including you, dear wife."

Mrs. Zeeman kissed her husband lightly. "Thank you. Listen, honey, after you pick up Grandma at the airport, could you take her out to dinner? I'm sure I'll be stuck at the dinner reception forever, okay?"

"Sure," Mr. Zeeman said. "But starting tomorrow, let's get some family time in around here, huh?"

"Deal," his wife said, kissing him lightly again. She looked at her watch. "I have to run. Okay, girls, let's get this wedding show on the road."

The girls lagged behind Breezy's mom so they'd have a moment alone to talk.

"I didn't sleep at all," Breezy whispered to her friends. "All night long I kept thinking I heard Hotdog scratching at the front door."

"I called the shelter again this morning," Cassie said, "just in case someone brought Hotdog back. He's not there."

"I should have been more careful when I tied his leash to that fence," Breezy insisted with tears in her eyes. "This is my fault!"

"Come on, Breezer, you can't blame yourself," Annie said, giving Breezy a quick hug. "We don't know what happened. Maybe Hotdog found a good home. Maybe — "

"Girls, it's now or never!" Mrs. Zeeman yelled up to them.

"Coming!" Breezy called back down.

They were silent all the way to the church. The only sound in the car was Tiffany's occasional yap of excitement as she watched the world go by out of the car window.

Breezy stared out the other window, unable to bring herself out of her funk.

I know we're working today, and I know I should be concentrating on taking care of Tiffany and little Wendy Anders and Michael Logan, but none of that seems important now. I vowed I'd take care of Hotdog, and I failed. I'm nothing but a big failure.

"Okay, girls, here you are," Mrs. Zeeman said, stopping the car in front of the church. "Annie, in case Mrs. Anders asks, Paula will be right over as soon as I get to the country club and take over there. We told Mrs. Anders three times yesterday, but she's liable to forget."

"Okay," Annie agreed.

"Thanks for the ride, Mom," Breezy said as she

and her friends got out of the car, Annie holding Tiffany in her arms.

Mrs. Zeeman stuck her head out the window to talk to Breezy. "I hope whatever is bothering you gets better, sweetie."

The ceremony wasn't scheduled to start for an hour, but Crystal wanted Tiffany in all the remaining wedding photos. Also, the girls were supposed to keep Wendy and Michael entertained before the ceremony, as well as afterward.

"Look, Breezy, they painted that fence where Hotdog was tied up yesterday," Cassie noted. The fence was now a glossy black. New lavender, deep purple, and white flowers had been planted in a border underneath it. More flowers in the same colors tumbled out of two huge urns right in front of the church. The flowers were the same colors as those Crystal had chosen for her wedding.

"Everything looks great," Breezy admitted forlornly. "The moms did a good job." She turned around and took a look down the street, hoping that by some stroke of luck she'd see Hotdog running toward her.

But the street was empty.

Tiffany ran in a circle around Breezy, wagging her tail happily. "She's trying to cheer you up," Annie told her.

"Thanks, Tiff," Breezy said with a sigh. She took one more look down the street in both directions. No Hotdog. "I guess we'd better go inside."

"Girls, thank heavens you're here!" Mrs. Anders cried as soon as she saw them. She looked very chic in a floor-length lavender and purple crepe dress with a matching jacket.

"We're right on time, Mrs. Anders," Annie pointed out politely.

"Yes, well, please follow me. Tiffany needs to go in there right away," she said, wringing her hands with anxiety. "And take charge of Wendy and Michael. Michael keeps trying to stuff wet tissues down Wendy's dress!"

The girls went into the sanctuary, where they found all the people in the wedding party milling around nervously. At the moment, the photographer was shooting pictures of Crystal and her parents. The girls knew Crystal's parents were divorced and her dad had finally decided to come in from Oregon for the wedding. Crystal stood between her parents, who clearly did not want to even look at each other.

Tom was standing near Crystal's brother, Pete, who was himself balanced on his crutches, flirting with the same tall, beautiful girl he'd been talking to the day before. The girl wore an elegantly simple lavender dress of raw silk that fell in a column to the floor.

"That girl with Pete is so beautiful," Cassie said dreamily. "I feel like I know her from somewhere."

"She's one of the bridesmaids," Annie said.

"Pete looks handsome in his tux," Cassie said.

"Don't get all crazy over him," Annie said. "He's the same guy who won't lift a pinky to help us with the canine beasts from hell."

Cassie smiled as her gaze switched to Tom. He had an awe-filled look on his face as he took in the sight of his radiant bride-to-be.

When the girls looked at Crystal, now being photographed just with Mrs. Anders, they understood why.

Crystal was a stunningly beautiful bride. Her wedding gown was very different from Liza's. Her ivory satin gown was simple and strapless, fitted to the body in one fluid line. But behind her, an attached train of the same ivory satin was covered with intricate lace. The lace was repeated in a wedding veil that fell backward from a crown of pearls that had been set into Crystal's upswept, shining blonde hair.

In her hands she held a small bouquet of baby roses in shades of white, ivory, and lavender.

"She's as beautiful as all of those supermodels," Cassie whispered reverentially. "She looks like an angel."

"Too bad she doesn't act like an angel," Annie whispered back.

"Now the bride alone, please," the photographer said.

"Could I have Tiffany, please?" Crystal asked, holding out her hands toward Annie.

Annie took the dog to Crystal. Crystal kissed Tiffany on her nose. "Thanks for taking such good care of her," Crystal told Annie.

Annie's jaw fell open in shock.

Had Crystal really just been *civil* to her?

"You're welcome," Annie said, backing away. "She's a cool pooch." She hurried over to her friends. "That can't be Crystal," she hissed in a low voice. "That had to be some really nice girl impersonating Crystal!"

"Have you ever seen a more beautiful bride?" Tom asked the girls as he walked over to them.

"No," Cassie said honestly.

"And she's as beautiful on the inside as she is on the outside," Tom added.

Annie gave him a look that said he was crazy.

"Oh, I guess she treated you to the Princess Crystal act, huh?" Tom figured out. "That's just a big front. She was convinced she was a geek in high school. All the popular girls told her she'd never make cheerleader. She's never forgotten how terrible they made her feel."

"But she was so pretty and so nice back then," Breezy exclaimed. "I wanted to grow up to be just like her!"

"And she's a *model*," Cassie added.

Tom shrugged. "I used to do a lot of fashion work. And believe it or not, some of the most beautiful models in the world are the most insecure." He craned his neck until he saw the tall girl who had been talking with Pete earlier.

"See her? Her name is Chandra Morris. She's Crystal's roommate — well, she was, anyway. Chandra makes a fortune in the business, but she still needs constant reassurance that she's attractive."

"You're kidding," Annie said. "When she looks like that?"

"Oh, my gosh, I do recognize her!" Cassie said with excitement. "She modeled in the last issue of *YM*. Do you think I could get her autograph?"

"Cassie, that is tacky in a major way," Annie said, making a face.

"I'm sure she'd love to be asked for her autograph," Tom said.

"Tom, could you join Crystal in the next shots, please?" the photographer's assistant called out.

"Sure," he called back. "Hey, Breezy?"

Breezy looked up. She had been lost in thought, trying to figure out how soon she'd be able to get away from the wedding to look for Hotdog. "What?"

"Don't forget to give me that address so I can send you your photos," Tom said as he walked away.

"Oh, thanks," Breezy said. She didn't care about the photos now. She didn't care about anything except finding that sweet, funny-looking dog.

"He's so nice," Cassie said dreamily. "He's almost as nice as David Silver. And almost as cute. And almost as wonderful, and . . ."

Someone standing behind Cassie cleared his throat.

No. It couldn't be. With her luck, it would be David Silver, and he would have heard what she just said.

Cassie turned around.

Yep. Her bad luck when it came to David was holding.

Because it was clear from the look on his face that he'd heard every single word.

33

"**D**avid," Cassie said, blushing a pink color much deeper than the dress she was wearing.

David was as red-faced as she was. He couldn't look her in the eye. But Melody, who was holding his hand, could.

"Cassie! You're in love with my brother!" she cried, jumping up and down. "I heard you!"

I want to die, Cassie thought. *Right now. This is so humiliating.*

"She didn't say she was in love," Annie said, jumping in for her friend. "She just said your brother is a nice guy, and he is."

David managed to lift his gaze after that. "Hi," he mumbled. "Uh . . . my parents wanted to come early, so . . . we're here. Early."

Breezy, who was still lost in thought, felt a tug on her hand. She looked down. There was Wendy Anders, in a miniature version of Crystal's wedding gown, except in light yellow. "Michael is being mean to me," she said. "I hate him."

"I hate you, too," Michael said, sticking his tongue out at her.

"Hey, you guys, that's not a nice thing to say," Cassie chided them.

"So? Who cares about nice?" Michael asked, pulling on the bottom of his tiny tuxedo jacket. He put his mouth on his arm and blew as hard as he could, making a very loud, very rude noise.

"Wendy cut one!" he then yelled as loud as he could.

This cracked Melody up. Wendy looked as if she was ready to cry.

"I did not," Wendy said with dignity, but then she hit Michael on the arm. "You stink."

"You stink worse!" Michael shot back.

"Let's go into the kids' lounge," Breezy said quickly. "We can do some fun stuff before the ceremony."

"I'm not going if she goes," Michael replied belligerently.

Tom came over to his nephew and crouched down. "Hey, big guy, remember how we talked about how we were both gonna act today?"

"Yeah," Michael admitted sheepishly, his head hanging.

"Okay, that's my guy," Tom said, putting out his hand palm up. "Gimme five. Today we both act like gentlemen all day long."

"Please, girls, take those kids out of here," Mrs. Anders told them, her hands fluttering nervously. "And whatever you do, make sure they stay neat!"

"Can I come, too?" Melody asked hopefully.

"Sure," Cassie told her.

Cassie was very happy when, without saying a word about it, David tagged along behind them. Maybe she hadn't ruined everything after all.

An hour later, the girls stood in the back of the lobby, keeping an eye on Wendy and Michael. A harpist wearing a flowing silver dress sat at the front of the sanctuary, playing heavenly music that indicated the wedding procession was about to begin. The sanctuary was full, and the bridal party stood in the lobby in order as Annie's mom hovered over them to make sure everyone was in place. The girls stood near Michael and Wendy, who would walk down the aisle before Crystal and her parents.

It was a beautiful day, quite hot, so the doors to the church were propped open to let in a breeze. Annie lifted her curly red hair, wishing she had on her baseball cap to keep her heavy hair off her neck.

Two by two, the members of the wedding party walked slowly down the aisle. The four brides-maids were in lavender silk dresses with purple satin around the neckline and the hem; each had a single purple gardenia in her hair. The grooms-men wore impeccably cut black tuxedos. All the guests craned their necks to watch the handsome procession move regally down the aisle. There was a good-natured chuckle when Pete came down the aisle on his crutches.

Then it was the maid of honor, Chandra, and Tom's best man, his cousin Larry from Detroit.

Cassie bent down to whisper in Michael's ear. "Okay, do you remember what you're supposed to do?"

"Yeah," Michael whispered back. "But I have to go to the bathroom."

"Well, you can't now," Annie hissed.

"I have to go to the bathroom, too," Wendy complained, twisting her little legs into a pretzel.

"Right after the ceremony," Cassie promised them. "Okay, you guys, remember to walk slowly."

Michael pulled his arm away when Wendy took it as they had practiced. She stomped her foot and grabbed it again, and this time he put up with it. The two of them walked down the aisle. Michael carried an ivory satin pillow that held the wedding rings. Wendy had a lavender basket on her arm, and she threw white rose petals out as she walked. There was an audible "Awww" from the assembled guests.

"So far, so good," Annie said, watching as the kids reached the front of the sanctuary.

"They're cute," Breezy said, trying to muster up enthusiasm that she just didn't feel.

Now Tom stood between his mom and dad, smiling first at one, then the other. Then the three of them walked down the aisle together. His tall, silver-haired parents looked regal, but his mom couldn't stop crying. When Tom and his parents got to the front of the sanctuary, Tom took out his handkerchief and tenderly wiped the tears from his mother's cheeks. That elicited another "Awwww" from the guests.

Then the music changed, and Crystal, standing between her estranged parents, began to walk down the aisle. Mrs. Anders led Tiffany along on a new lavender leash, and the dog was on perfect behavior. There was an audible gasp at Crystal's beauty. Cassie got teary-eyed. Even Annie felt a tiny lump in her throat.

Maybe marriage wouldn't be that terrible, she thought. *If I wait until I'm really old. And if I can find a guy who loves sports and adventure as much as I do. But he sure better never, ever try and tell me what to do!*

"Dearly beloved, we are gathered together for the wonderful occasion of the joining of Thomas Spencer Logan and Crystal Elizabeth Anders in holy matrimony," the minister said.

"They look so beautiful together, don't they?" Cassie whispered to her friends from the back of the church.

"How can you tell? Their backs are to you," Annie said. She fanned her neck. "Man, it's hot in here." She looked over at Breezy, who was looking toward the open door of the church instead of watching the wedding. Annie knew that Breezy's mind was completely on the missing Hotdog.

"It'll be okay, Breezer," Annie assured her. "As soon as our job is over, we'll go search for Hotdog. And we won't quit until we find him."

Breezy shook her head no. "It'll be too late by then," she said sadly. "I'm such a terrible person. I should be out there right now — "

"It isn't your fault, I keep telling you that," Annie insisted.

"Then why do I feel like it is?" Breezy asked.

"You guys, we have to watch the wedding," Cassie hissed, admonishing them. "We're working!"

Breezy knew Cassie was right. She turned away from the open door and forced herself to focus on the wedding ceremony. Clearly, she had already missed quite a bit of it.

". . . And do you, Thomas Spencer Logan, take this woman to be your lawfully wedded wife, in sickness and in health, in good times and in bad, will you cleave to her until death do you part?"

"I do," Tom said firmly. He took the wedding ring from the satin pillow that Michael held and winked at his little nephew. Michael winked back.

Everyone laughed, and then got teary-eyed as Tom put the ring on Crystal's finger. Even from the back of the church, the girls could see that there were tears of joy in Crystal's eyes.

"Marriage is a sacred union," the minister said. "I've known you, Crystal, since you were a little girl singing in the children's chorus here at our church. I remember how you hated to get your dress dirty when you went with the other kids to play in what was then our new church playground." He smiled at her fondly.

"The years have flown by, Crystal, and now you're a grown woman, a beautiful, successful model living in New York City. Everyone back here in Summerville is so proud of all that you have accomplished. . . ."

The minister went on and on. At first it was sweet, but after a while it was just endless. The church grew hotter and hotter. People were fanning themselves with whatever they could find.

". . . And then there was the time when you were twelve, Crystal, and you decided you wanted to be a cheerleader. . . ."

"Cancel the honeymoon, this wedding is going to last forever!" Annie whispered to Cassie. "We should have brought a sack dinner and a sleeping bag."

"And then, Crystal, there was high school . . ."

From behind the girls, they heard a loud,

startling bark. Everyone in the sanctuary heard it, too, and they all turned around, grateful for any distraction from the droning minister.

Another loud bark, and a mass of filthy brown canine fur streaked by the girls, heading for the wedding party.

"Hotdog!" Breezy yelled with joy when she realized who the brown streak of fur actually was. "It's Hotdog!"

34

Clearly, Hotdog had found his way back to the church, where the girls had left him the day before, and had bounded into the church through the open doors.

It was also clear that the dog, who was about as dirty as a stray dog could get, was headed straight for the wedding party.

Acting on pure instinct, Annie ran like a flash down the aisle after the sprinting Hotdog. She took a running leap and managed to tackle the dog just before Hotdog's muddy paws hit Crystal's wedding gown. Cradling the dog in her arms, she held him like a football, landing on the train to Crystal's elegant dress.

R-i-i-i-p.

Everyone heard it. Crystal gasped.

Slowly Annie got up, holding the squirming Hotdog in her arms. Crystal's train was no longer attached to her wedding gown. In fact, there was a large rip up the back of the dress.

Everyone just stood there in shock. Even the minister couldn't speak.

"I am so sorry," Annie managed to squeak out.

"Give Hotdog to me," Breezy said. She and Cassie had run down the aisle to help. Now Breezy held her hands out for the dog.

Annie put Hotdog in Breezy's arms, but somehow the dog managed to squirm out of her grasp. Hotdog barked happily and ran down the aisle toward the open door again. Mrs. Anders was in such a state of shock that she momentarily forgot to hold fast to Tiffany's leash, and the little poodle went bounding after Hotdog.

"This is a disaster!" Mrs. Anders cried. "Get Tiffany! Get that mutt out of here!"

The crowd began to buzz about this bizarre state of affairs. Many of the wedding guests laughed heartily as Hotdog pranced away from the playful Tiffany, waited until Tiffany almost caught him, then pranced away again.

The girls tried their best to capture both dogs, and Mrs. McGee got into the act, too, but both dogs ran outside before they could be grabbed.

"Surround them!" Annie instructed. "Go the other way, Cassie!" Cassie ran by the newly painted black fence. The dogs were running away from Annie and Breezy and toward her. Somehow Hotdog got by her, but she thought she had a shot at catching Tiffany. She reached down and caught the edge of one poodle puffball, but the tiny dog squirmed away.

Off-balance, Cassie brushed the fence.

The paint was still wet. Now there was black glossy paint all over the front of her pale pink dress. She reached down to touch it. And then the palms of her hands were black.

"I got him, I got him!" Annie cried triumphantly as she managed to scoop Hotdog up near an oak tree across the street.

"And I got Tiffany!" Breezy said.

By this time many of the people from the wedding were standing on the front steps of the church, watching the antics. They applauded happily when they saw that the two dogs had been captured at last. Annie handed Hotdog to Breezy and Breezy handed Tiffany to Annie. Breezy kissed Hotdog all over.

"Get back into the church this instant!" Mrs. Anders commanded from the door to the church. Her voice was vibrating with rage.

"We are in so much trouble," Cassie whispered to her friends.

"Mrs. McGee, I'll take this up with you later," Mrs. Anders told Annie's mother ominously. Mrs. McGee's face was the color of typing paper. She looked like she was going to faint.

"It'll be okay, Mom," Annie assured her mother as she hurried by with Tiffany.

Breezy and Cassie tried to smile at Mrs. McGee as they hurried back into the sanctuary. Breezy held Hotdog tightly in her arms, and Annie handed Tiffany's leash to Mrs. Anders. The wedding party took their places again and the guests went back to their seats.

Frankly, everyone except Mrs. Anders was in a much better mood now. People were laughing and exclaiming over the excitement, instead of fanning themselves from the heat and the boredom of the minister's long-winded remarks.

"Shall we continue?" the minister asked, blotting his forehead with his handkerchief.

Breezy was overjoyed that Hotdog was back, but she felt terrible over the mess she had created. It was her fault that Crystal's wedding was ruined! Her eyes slid over to the bride. Crystal's head was down and her shoulders were shaking.

She's crying, Breezy realized, *and it's all my fault. I have to do something!*

"Excuse me, Reverend," Breezy said, her knees shaking with nerves. "I just want to apologize to Crystal and Tom and . . . well, everyone, for disrupting the wedding. It was my fault."

She took a deep breath and gathered up all her nerve. "You see, this dog — me and my friends named him Hotdog — well, he's homeless. And the shelter was going to put him to sleep because they don't have enough funding to take care of the animals. We couldn't just let him die."

290

Hotdog gave her face a loving slurp. "I mean, I know he's funny-looking," Breezy continued, "and he's not glamorous and he doesn't have a pedigree like Tiffany. But he doesn't have to pretend to be anything he isn't to get me and my friends to love him. We think he's perfect just the way he is. Anyway, I'm really sorry, and . . . I guess that's all I wanted to say."

Breezy went to stand with the disheveled Annie and the paint-dappled Cassie. The three of them were ready to accept whatever punishment would be meted out. Whatever it turned out to be, they would be in it together. As one, they looked at the bride and groom. Crystal's head was bowed, clearly in anger and sadness at her wedding having been ruined.

Finally, Crystal lifted her head. There were tears in her eyes.

But incredulously, the girls realized that they weren't tears of sadness, they were tears of mirth.

Crystal had been laughing!

"Crystal?" her mother asked uncertainly. "Are you okay?"

Crystal burst into a peal of laughter. That made everyone in the sanctuary laugh with her. Tom gave her a huge, approving hug.

"I'll tell you this much," Crystal said, wiping the tears from her eyes. "No one will ever, *ever* forget my wedding day!"

"And I am the luckiest guy on earth to be marrying you," Tom told her tenderly. He took her hands in his, and looked into her eyes. "I know we decided not to write our own wedding vows, but there's something that I want to say to you, in front of all of our family and friends. Crystal, I love you exactly as you are. The real Crystal, not the glamorous model. It's kind of like that funny-looking dog. You never have to be anything but who you really are with me. Because who you really are is perfect."

"You guys, he means he doesn't care if she's a fashion model or not," Cassie whispered to her friends. "Oh, this is the most romantic thing I ever saw in my life."

"I love you, too," Crystal said. She turned and her eyes locked on Breezy. "Is that funny-looking dog still homeless?"

Everyone turned to look at Breezy. She nodded yes.

"Well, I think Tiffany needs a playmate. Tom and I will adopt him," she said. "And I promise, no rhinestone collar."

There was another huge "Awww" from the guests, and Tom hugged Crystal again. Then he turned to the flabbergasted minister. "With all due respect, sir, could you just wrap things up now? We have to go buy some dog biscuits."

Everyone laughed, even the minister. "I must say, this is the most . . . unique wedding I ever had the privilege of performing. I now pronounce you husband and wife," he said. "You may kiss the bride."

Tom took Crystal into his arms and swooped her backward so that her veil touched the floor, not far from the torn train. Then he gave her the tenderest, most loving kiss in the world.

The harpist began to play, and a jubilant Tom and his new bride, radiant Crystal Logan with the ripped wedding gown, walked up the aisle arm in arm.

The rest of the wedding party followed the bridal couple out. They formed a receiving line on the steps in front of the church. The guests began to leave their seats. People were laughing and crying from happiness at the hilarity and beauty of the wedding they had just witnessed.

"Do you realize what a major bullet we just dodged?" Annie asked. "This fiasco could have put us out of the wedding business forever." She ruffled Hotdog's fur. "And it's all your fault!"

"Maybe it still will," Cassie said nervously, craning her neck toward the receiving line. "After all, Mrs. Anders is the one who hired us. And she's super-mad."

Breezy kissed Hotdog on the top of his head. "I wish I could keep him."

"After what just happened, you'll be lucky if your parents keep you," Cassie said. She looked down at her dress. "My mom is going to kill me for ruining this dress. I don't think you can get paint out of velvet."

"Cassie?"

She turned around. Of course it was David. For once, Melody wasn't with him.

"Every time I see you something awful happens," Cassie said, making a face at her filthy dress.

He smiled a sweet, crooked smile. "Maybe I'm a jinx."

"Or maybe I'm a klutz," Cassie sighed ruefully.

David stuck his hands in his pockets. "So, I'll see you at the reception, huh?"

"Sure," Cassie said. "I'll just pretend that my dress was pink and black the whole time."

He grinned at her. "Cool. Save me a dance." He turned and hurried away.

"Wow!" Cassie cried, grabbing Breezy's and Annie's hands. "Did you hear that? Did you hear how normal I sounded when I talked to him?"

"You are so improved," Annie told her.

"And maybe we can all go out together! On a picnic to Wagner Lake. He wants me to! Of course, if I tell my parents there's a guy involved, they'll think it's a date and they won't let me go."

"It *is* a date," Breezy pointed out.

"It's a group date," Cassie corrected. "Well, I'll think of something. Because you know my parents. They say I can't date until I'm in college or something."

"Hey, girls!" Chandra said, coming down the aisle to them. "I didn't get a chance to meet you yet. I'm Chandra Morris. I'm — "

"We know who you are," Cassie said with excitement. "I saw photos of you in *YM*. You're famous!"

"Well, thanks," Chandra said. "Anyway, Crystal asked me to come in and get Hotdog. She wants the photographer to get a shot of her new doggie. And then she said she'd like you to take both dogs to Pete's before the reception."

"I'll bring him right out," Breezy assured her. Chandra went back out to the receiving line.

Breezy looked down at the dog in her arms. Hotdog gave her another loving lick. "I guess this is good-bye," she told him. Her eyes filled with tears.

That made Cassie's eyes fill with tears, too. "At least you found him a home, Breezy," she said softly. "That's the most important thing."

"I know," Breezy said. "And I know I'm being selfish. But . . ." She tried to gulp back her tears. "It's so hard to say good-bye to someone you love."

Annie gave Hotdog a hug and a kiss, then Cassie did, too.

"I'll be right back," Breezy said. "I'm going to take Hotdog to his new owners."

Breezy walked outside into the bright sunshine. Mrs. Anders was talking to a group of people on the sidewalk, Tiffany's leash clasped firmly in her hand. Pete was monopolizing Chandra again. Breezy waited until the last guests had finished kissing Crystal and congratulating Tom, and then she went over to them. Wordlessly, she handed Hotdog to Crystal.

"You love this dog, don't you?" Crystal said kindly.

Breezy nodded. She knew if she spoke, she'd start crying.

Crystal handed Hotdog to Tom, then turned back to Breezy. "Listen, I know I wasn't very nice to you and your friends. And I'm sorry. I . . ." She looked over at Tom, who gave her a loving look. "Well, let's just say that I heard what you said about Hotdog. And I heard what Tom said about me. I acted like an idiot. Frankly, I didn't even like me."

Breezy nodded again.

"You were a great kid to baby-sit for, Breezy. And you turned into a great teenager. I just want you to know that."

"Thanks."

Crystal smiled. "Hey, listen, I get back to Summerville at least a couple of times a year. How about if when I come home to visit Mom, I bring Hotdog? You can see him all you want."

"Really?" Breezy asked. "Do you mean it?"

"Absolutely," Crystal said. "So this won't be good-bye, it'll just be good-bye for now."

Tom put his arm around Crystal's shoulder. "Now, see, this is the Crystal I fell in love with." He tenderly kissed her cheek.

The photographer quickly snapped some photos of Crystal and Tom with Hotdog, who posed as if he'd been doing it all his life.

"Breezy, where are your partners?" Mrs. Anders asked, hurrying over to them. "My Crystal doesn't want that mangy dog all over her and Tom now. Goodness, he's probably shedding all over the two of you!"

"We're fine, Mom," Crystal said.

"You're not really adopting that . . . that *thing*, are you?"

"We just did," Tom said. "But Breezy is going to take Hotdog and Tiffany over to Pete's now."

Mrs. Anders handed over Tiffany's leash. "I think you have lost your minds," she said. "What kind of famous New York model owns a mutt? What would *People* say?"

"Mom, I'm not a famous model," Crystal said. "So just get over it. I'm certainly trying to."

Breezy took the two dogs back into the sanctuary, where her friends were still waiting.

"Crystal said she'd bring Hotdog when she comes home to visit," Breezy told them. "Outside just now, she was . . . she was just like how she used to be."

She reached for Tiffany's leash. "It's stupid to pretend to be something you're not. If people don't like you for your real self, then too bad for them." Out from the neckline of her sweater, she pulled the small silver key she always wore. "That's why I'm always going to wear this, you guys. Because the three of us never have to be fake with each other, ever."

Cassie and Breezy pulled out their keys, too. They all smiled at each other.

"Do you think the moms will ever hire us to help at a wedding after this?" Breezy asked. "I messed up everything so badly."

"Oh, Breezy, you're way too hard on yourself," Cassie said. "Everything turned out great after all."

"And if the moms do get mad, all three of us are taking the blame," Annie added. "One for all and all for one."

Breezy smiled at Annie. "You two are the two best friends in the world."

"Especially me," Annie joked. "I am, like, so cool."

Cassie crossed her fingers and shut her eyes tight. "I'm making a wish."

"There's no shooting star in here, Cass," Annie said.

"I don't care, I'm making a special wish, anyway," she said, not opening her eyes. "I wish that all of our dreams would come true. And we all live happily ever after."

"And stay best friends," Breezy added. "Forever."

"Forever," Cassie and Annie agreed.

Hotdog barked in agreement, and so did Tiffany. The girls laughed. Then they led the dogs outside and headed for Pete's house, best friends forever, always there for each other, to help make their wishes come true.

ABOUT THE AUTHOR

Cherie Bennett enjoys writing fun novels for young readers, like *The Wedding That Almost Wasn't*, as well as more serious literature. She is one of America's finest young playwrights: Her *Anne Frank & Me* was a recent New York hit, while her *Cyra & Rocky* was presented at The Kennedy Center. She also authors the "Hey, Cherie!" teen advice column, syndicated nationally by Copley News Service. Her other Scholastic titles include *Girls in Love* and *The Bridesmaids*.

Cherie may be contacted at P.O. Box 150326, Nashville, TN 37215, or by E-mail at author-chik@aol.com.